Chaya's First Death

The Beginning of an End to her life as an Enabler!

By: A. *Life* Gant

Chaya's First Death

This book is a work of fiction. Names, characters, places, and incidents are the product of the author's imagination or are used fictitiously. Any resemblance to actual events, locales, or persons, living or dead, is coincidental.

Unless otherwise noted, Scriptures are taken from the King James Version of the Bible.

Copyright © 2007 by A. Life Gant and Eborya Enterprises, LLC
All rights reserved.

No part of this book may be reproduced in any form or by any electronic or mechanical means, including information storage and retrieval systems, without permission in writing from the author and/or publisher, except by a reviewer who may quote brief passages in a review. The intent of the author is only to offer information of a general nature to help you in your quest for emotional and spiritual well-being. In the event you use any of the information in this book for yourself, which is your constitutional right, the author and the publisher assume no responsibility for your actions.

Eborya Publishing
a division of Eborya Enterprises, LLC
P.O. BOX 33044 Tulsa, Ok 74153-1044
Visit our Web site at www.Eborya.com

Cover design by Dee Gaymon- info@ktisis-online.com
Printed in the United States of America

ISBN: 978-1-60530-434-2

A. *Life* Gant

For My Daughters

Chaya's First Death

<u>Acknowledgements</u>

First of all, I must thank My Heavenly Father, My Lord and Savior, Jesus Christ. For it is in Him that I live, breathe, move, and write. Without you Lord, I know exactly where I would be: **Lost!** Your precious Spirit gave me the ability to put pen to paper and express my innermost. Although there were times I wanted to quit because the pain became too much, You reminded me that it is not about me, it's all about souls and the healing of them. If you could die for me that I might be free, then I must die to myself, through the release of my writing to free someone else and For This Lord, I Give You Praise!

To my family, every last one of you! There are too many names to list. Thank you all for having been an instrument in some part of my life, good or bad, because without experience and having gone through something, change is next to impossible. I love you all!

Bernie, we could have never experienced the warmth of true sunshine, if we didn't have a little rain, or should I say, Thunderstorms! I love you!

Eboni and Arya, as Mama is writing these words, with tears flowing down my face, I say thank you girls, continuously! Having you two in my life has caused me to push when I didn't want to, pray when I didn't feel like it, and be a mother when I didn't know how. Babies, you will never know how much mommy loves you. I thank God for you. Mama did this one especially for you, just to let you know that you don't have to ever experience what I've had to go through when you are older. The chain is broken and although you might get hit by a link or two, it will never, ever, be able to bind you! Mama loves you both with all the love I have in me!

A. *Life* Gant

To Momma, my late grandmother, Mary P. Thompson, if it had not been for you...Need I say more? Besides, we talk all the time, so I am just going to say on paper that I Love You and Thank God for You!

To my own mother, Charlesetta M. Thompson, Thank You! If ever there was a time that I have failed to say it, I will say it again, Thank You! We've been through much, but we have come out and are still coming out; Victorious! Just so you know, as a mother, a friend, and a confidante, You're Irreplaceable! I Love You!

To all of you who I can't list by name, My friends, clients, innocent bystanders (LOL), Thank You All and I Love You!

To the one who believes she has rights...(lol) Mrs. 'Chaunda Pete, first of all, I say thank you! Your words of encouragement when we have our little talks, were one of the catalysts that pushed me to share a part of my story in this book. There were many others that may have made suggestions but God knew at that time, what I needed to hear to get me to move. Girl, You kinda' alright! (lol) No seriously, I love you and thank God for you allowing Him to use you as a vessel, whether you knew it or not!

Kendal, Kendal , Kendal....Mrs. Turner, I love you and thank God for you! Joka' had it not been for the Lord in you helping me with the much needed information to write and publish this book, ... Man! Your wealth of knowledge gave me the wind my wings needed to fly and keep flying!

Now this one is to the enemy and all his sidekicks! I thank you all the most because if it had not been for you causing me pain, holding me back, and delaying my promises, I would have never been able to fulfill My Destiny! Ha! You thought you had me but guess what? I got away!

~A.LifeGant

Chaya's First Death

Foreword

Today in America and around the world, they are so many women who are abused; emotionally, mentally, physically, and psychologically. So often they have been and are still crying out for help, when no one seemingly can hear them. In this book, **A.** *Life* **Gant**, displays and represents the anguish and reality of the character, which speaks for the majority of women in America and the world abroad.

Chaya's First Death demonstrates a family woman, caring and loving, who wanted to see her family prosper. She tried to practice everything as a Christian woman should. She did all she could, gave her all, went above and beyond, yet it seemed as though she had not yet began. On the outside looking in, a woman as such would appear to be donning the crown of superwoman. The correct title for her would actually be 'Codependent' or 'Enabler'. Although being this way comes easy for people who look out for the well-being of others before themselves, it can be very dangerous.

Like so many women and people today, the portrayed character lied to herself, remaining in a constant state of denial, wanting to believe that things were going to get better, when all the signs of a complete disastrous shipwreck were evident. Those same women also hold on to broken relationships as long as possible because what is really wanted or sought after is a change. They have become so accustomed to disorder in the past as children, and now as adults, that any kind of change would do. Chaya finally realized as we must, that there is a cycle to everything and depending on its course, it may or may not have to be broken. As my folks always say, "it is not the very same day the bucket goes to the well that the bottom will fall out." This book is quite captivating and interesting. It represents the life and story of a character on the verge of a much needed, non-physical death, to share with the world that there is life beyond the grave. I speak for the majority, strongly recommend, an endorse this book. I believe that it could be produced into plays and light up the big screens as well!

-Dr. Paul O-A Powell
Author, Publicist, Producer, Songwriter and Sole Entrepreneur

A. *Life* Gant

"Let Me Outta Here! Please! Somebody? Anybody? Let Me Out!" Chaya cried until she couldn't cry anymore. She screamed until she couldn't say a word. When she realized that no one was responding to her pleas, Chaya became overwhelmed with anger. So much so, that she began to kick the door, praying it would open. "Ugh! Ugh!" Still kicking. "I, Ugh! Am, Ugh! Ready, Ugh! To, Ugh! Gooo! Ugh!" That one last kick should have done it, she thought. But her feet swelled with pain. Her desire for release was so great that apparently she had forgotten the institution removed her shoes the moment she walked through the doors.

Chaya was exhausted. Her rampage exerted every ounce of energy in her body. By now, the bed looked appealing. How could she resist a twin bed with a bare mattress and box spring? Blankets and sheets were never issued to patients like her. Smart. Funny. Attractive. But mentally unstable. Patients like her knew everything, yet they didn't know anything. When they were on the outside, no one could tell what was going on in their heads. They smiled. Dressed well. Went to church. Had a decent job. The house and the car. Got married and had children.

To look at Chaya you wouldn't know that she was a ticking time bomb. A cataclysmic event on the verge of an explosion.

Curled up in a fetal position, barefoot and out of her mind, Chaya rocked herself to sleep. Asleep but awake. Her body lay limp and lifeless, but her mind paced the floor of her head. She slept but didn't rest. Chaya lay there for what seemed like hours to her, but actually was only moments. Her eyes popped open and she sat up. Realizing again where she was, the fight was on! Her voice had had a long enough break.

"Let Me Out! Please Release Me! Somebody? Anybody?" Chaya began her kick and scream fest all over again. The padded walls prevented her from injuring herself completely. She continued in this manner for hours, that turned into days. One of

Chaya's First Death

which, the orderlies came in and bound her with a straight jacket. She tried to free herself, 'Incredible Hulk-style,' but the straps only got tighter.

She grunted over and over until it happened... She stopped. Abruptly. The square room was spinning as if on an axis. Her head hurt. Not the type of headaches she was accustomed to. No. This one was different. It felt like someone was squeezing her brains in a play-dough fashion.

"What's happening to me? Why won't anybody help me? I'm tired. Tired." She whispered that last word. Tears found their way back to her face and rolled onto the sheetless mattress. If anyone knew what being tired meant, it was Chaya. "Lord, I am Tired!"

Suddenly, the room's spin came to a screeching halt. Although confined in white, she began to feel a little more freedom. More than before. Chaya allowed her body to relax.

"I will keep you in perfect peace..."

Her almond-shaped eyes grew to the size of silver dollars, displaying recognition. Her memory began to be kind to it's owner. She finished the verse. "Whose mind is stayed on thee!" Happily, she shouted this verse as loud, maybe louder, than her pleas for help.

Afraid to enter her room, those same workers peeked through the one inch window. Their minds could not conceive what was going on. How had this thing happened? Turning away from one another, they simultaneously peeked again. Something had changed in that room. There was a light shining upon her but no light bulb was in the room. The same woman whose visage was severely distorted. The look in her eyes were dim. Now, she was smiling and crying all at the same time. She was more free in the straight jacket then she had been in years. Confined yet Free.

"I will keep you in perfect peace whose mind is stayed on thee."

Chaya came to herself. "That's my daddy talking to me!"

A. *Life* Gant

She spoke of her Heavenly Father. "I hear you Lord."
    While she listened to what He had to say, that play-dough feeling, intensified. He was shaping, re-making, and molding her mind to one that was like His. He reminded her that she was not the first one and certainly wouldn't be the last to go through a situation of this caliber.
    Now the Word on reserve, became a wellspring of living water that flooded her soul. Chaya engulfed herself in the Word. The Word that she remembered. Recalling Psalms 23, she, as the old folks say, "Got Happy." Chaya, "got happy" at every phrase, but a few of them really touched her soul.
    ...He maketh me to lie down in green pastures... She prayed that her literal bed of pain, shame and guilt, would become as those same green pastures.
    ...He leadeth me beside the still waters... "Lord, I thank You for giving me the kind of peace that is as still as the waters."
    ...He restoreth my soul... Chaya was speechless. Her tear-filled faced, spoke restoration. No more would she allow anybody or anything, cause her to lose her joy, her peace, and certainly not her mind.
    She closed her eyes and rested.
    Night had fallen and the light from the stars tapped on her window pane. They were bidding her farewell and wishing her sweet dreams. She could have sworn that she heard one of them speaking audibly:
    "Weeping may endure for a night but Joy cometh...

Chaya's First Death

"It's morning Momma! Time to get Up!" Each of their taps grew louder than the last. Rising to a seated position at the side of her bed, free from the straight jacket of life, she silently thanked the Lord. Thanked Him for keeping her mind, even when she lost it herself. Chaya smiled at her girls and returned the greeting. "Good Morning Babies."

Dressed and ready to go. Not caring who got left behind, she yelled to the occupants of her house. "It's time to go!" Chaya drove the kids to school and dropped her husband off at work. His car was broken down again! But she couldn't worry about that because she was determined to stay, in her "Morning!"

A. *Life* Gant

Introduction

"I'm a mother and do you think I am going to sit here and allow my kids to go without?"
Crazy can not be just a part of your character, it must be Your name!

~~~~~~~~~~~~

There is a time and place for a woman to do whatever it takes to make sure she and her kids have all the necessary things to survive. This includes the usual food, clothes, shelter, lights, gas, water and transportation. Of course, when you as a woman are a 'sho'nuf momma or should I say, a real mother, the phrase 'Time and Place' doesn't exist. The terms like 'whenever or whatever', 'any and everything' far supersedes painful realizations stated as: "My children will go hungry." "My child needs new shoes." or "That shirt doesn't need to be ironed!"(in lieu of the fact that the electric had been shut off!)

Chaya was raised by strong women, physically and mentally. Some folks called them rebellious, ignorant, and silly, to name a few. Today, the word independent is widely used and sometimes on a first name basis. For example, "I am an independent, strong, black woman whose name happens to be..." However, her upbringing has a lot, if not all, to do with her agenda or should we say problem.

Chaya's First Death

"Hold your head up high when you walk!" "Stick your chest out with every step you take!" "Be proud of who you are!" "Never be ashamed of where you come from!" "Do whatever it takes to make it!" "Take time to stop and smell the roses!" The list can go on but the all too familiar ones that ring the most truth are: "Let nothing or no one tell you what you can't do!" "Never let a man live with you for free and should they try, make sure they Never forget...One thing...You can do bad all by yourself!"

Of course being taught how to be independent, is and can be a great thing but it can also become detrimental to you as well as others connected to you. Thoughts like, 'You can't tell me what to do!', 'I don't need you!', and or ' I can do it myself!', ring loud in do-it-yourselfers. While some statements may be factual, most, definitely do not equal truth! Everybody needs somebody and regardless of what most people think, you may even need more than one somebody! Which brings me to the reason for sharing Chaya's story. I hope you can sit back, relax with a cup of your favorite beverage, occasionally laugh or cry a bit with her, but ultimately, learn from her mistakes, for they have and will become Victories (for you and her)!

~~~~~~~~~~~~~~~~~~~~

Chaya often wondered why she had to go through some, if not all of the things she went through as a child up until now.

Being raised in an unfit environment for most of her childhood certainly was not one of her desires. The needs of the house were taken care of as much as possible and there was lack all the way around but that is not to say her upbringing was at all times sad. Of course there were times when her and her sibling's faces held nothing but smiles. Happiness was distributed throughout their home in sporadic proportions. Holidays and birthdays were always a treat because gifts took the place of any previous bouts of sadness. Dolls, combs and brushes, construction

A. *Life* Gant

paper and crayons, replaced tears and frustration, temporarily.
    "What is wrong with you and why are your lips poked out?", her mother asked her quite often.
    The responses were hardly ever sufficient enough to excuse her behind from a whooping.
    "I don't know," she replied.
    But that was truly what she believed, despite what she felt! Her demeanor was commonly referred to by Dinah, her mother as "an attitude!"
    Chaya could not remember very many times when she didn't have one! An attitude.... because somebody came in her room, touched her stuff, bothered her, or even looked at her crazy, or maybe it was because of something a whole lot deeper! As time went on, she realized it was the latter.

    Now pay attention to Chaya's story. It could be yours or somebody's you know and it may be useful for deliverance. If Chaya can come out, anybody can!

Chaya's First Death

Chapter One

"Momma, I wanna be a cheerleader!"
With each practice, the girls gained more confidence in the steps and the cheers became routine. Coy and Beta celebrated the mere idea that becoming a part of the squad was evident.
"Shake, shake, 1-2-3. Shake, shake, 1-2-3."
Her daughters were really shaking their hips. Even if one was a little stiff. She laughed to herself. Chaya was present at every single practice so she too could learn the material. Keeping count in her head wasn't difficult because as their mother, she knew recollection was in order. Looking great at doing moves fit for tiny tots was out of the question and besides, she did not have a care in the world! Her kids' rhythm was at stake and to leave them unprepared in a world full of below the belt movement was not happening!
"Momma, like this? Is this the right way to do it?"
In an effort to assist the coach in molding the sharp twists and turns of the hips, Chaya led her daughters in what hopefully appeared to be an exact replica of the artwork practiced on Monday.
A few rehearsals caused time to move swiftly until the Day of Reckoning.
"It's gone cost one hundred and ninety dollars! Momma that's a whole bunch of dollars! Do you have a lot of money? Momma, how much money do you have? One hundred ninety dollars for me and my sister?"

A. *Life* Gant

Time seemed to have wings during practices until it came to a screeching halt at the next question answer combo bolted out by Beta, her baby girl.

"Momma, if it costs so much, will we still get to be cheerleaders? And plus, you can have our money!"

Coy was a saver and she saved all the monies she received from any occasion. But now her little sister had already begun to follow suit and she offered all she had to her mother. She was the main one who wanted to become a cheerleader in the first place.

"Baby, don't worry about it. God will make a way and if I can, I'll try my best to get the money."

Chaya prayed and asked the Lord to make a way.

" Lord, It is hard to be a good mother during times like these and I know that You can and will make a way. So I'm thanking You in advance! I believe it and I receive it right now in Jesus' name".

Prayer was just what she needed and she always felt better afterwards.

"Go upstairs, make sure your rooms are clean and quit asking about being cheerleaders! Ain't nobody got four hundred dollars to give away like that!"

The girls were saddened at the words their daddy spoke and their mother wondered why he said what he said in such a harsh tone. Chaya tried her best not to say anything about his statements. She just kept her thoughts to herself.

"As if he would or could help anyway. He's just saying that because he knows he can't pay for it."

Regardless of the statements made by her male counterpart, Chaya still purposed in her heart to make sure her babies were not disappointed again, for it had become all too common.

"Did you say your prayers, brush your teeth and wash your face this morning? Make sure you get some lotion on those ashy body parts, especially the visible ones!"

~15~

Chaya's First Death

"Momma what's visible?" Beta asked.
"The parts you can see girl, now speed it up because you all will be late for school again!" Chaya exclaimed. The tardiness factor was a whole other issue, of course she wasn't the driver.
Beta, the youngest girl, began what she thought was a speedy transition from being naked and shoeless to fully clothed from head to.....
"Wait a minute! What is wrong with your shoe?" Chaya was ready to blow her top. When it came to her children and their welfare, hell couldn't stand against her.
"It has a hole in it." The seven year-old said sadly.
"Go take it off and put on some more shoes!"
Instantly, Chaya became inwardly disappointed, frustrated, and angry all at once. Her temples resembled bass-filled speakers. That was a straw she considered to be the next to the next to the last one, and she meant that!
Being married but yet living as one who leads a single life had become all too real and was not the plan she knew to be purposed in her life! Yet she pressed on! She had to do something about her baby's shoe situation. Who else could Chaya count on? She was the go to person in her family and there were no shoulders for her to cry on! She was the shoulder!
Oh well! Thank God her little girl had other decent shoes to wear. Not that Beta wore the ones most logical. Of course, she decided to jam her tootsies into a pair that fit to a tee. There was no need to even wonder what pair she chose. Beta ran and picked out her favorite, too little pair!
Still Chaya's head ached and her heart yearned for the needs of her children that she seemingly could not provide.

"Hey Momma, the Get a Grip is here. Can we go? The school gave us a coupon and it only costs a dollar!"
Coy, Chaya's oldest daughter, spoke of the state fair, whose slogan was 'Get a Grip'.

A. *Life* Gant

"I don't know baby, maybe grandma will take you, since she usually takes you guys every year." This was all Chaya could think of to say, as her daughter kept badgering her about going to the fair.

"I hope so Momma, because all my friends are going and I wanna go too." Coy was adamant, and for this reason, Chaya remained in a constant state of perseverance.

"I know, but if grandma doesn't take you, I'll see if we can go when I make some more money at the salon."

"Okay." Coy said in response to her mother's slightly raised tone of voice. But it was not the end of that conversation by no means.

Days passed and Chaya believed being on the hook was done away with, until one morning, while getting the girls dressed for school, a commercial came on about special discounts the fair was offering, and the flame was rekindled!

"Momma, can we gooo... please, please, pleeease!?"

Now both of her kids were begging to go. All she could do was pray and try her best to make some extra money to take them. The pleading continued and her heart sank deeper into the beginning stages of depression. Trying to control her tension-filled tone of voice, she just bolted out an answer.

"Don't worry, I said, we'll see! Just give Momma a chance to get some money together!"

This phrase too, had become just another group of words turned into a broken promise, again one she thought she could keep.

"Lord, I trust that you've got it all under control."

Chaya did indeed trust her heavenly father because after all, He was there at all times, whether it was when she thought she needed Him or not.

She did have a couple of friends she would talk to when she felt a need for human contact.

"Hhmp! Let me call Chastity to see what she is doing."

Chaya's First Death

    Chaya picked up her cordless telephone and dialed her best friend's number.
    "Hello? Hellooo?"
    Chaya's girlfriend Chastity, definitely couldn't hear a thing when she was on that cell phone of hers.
    "Chas' can you hear me now?"
    That girl has known that she needed a new phone. The flip phone she had was jacked up! Chaya smiled and thought to herself before answering her friend's question.
    "Chay? Is that you? You know how this thing acts?"
    To Chaya, other than her baby sister Daya, Chastity was the next best thing to having another sister. They chatted about whatever the other needed or wanted to talk about and the issues on mothering was no exception.
    "Hey Chas' what are you doing?"
    "Nothing. What's up? You alright?"
    Chastity was great at being there to listen to her best friend because she had gone through a similar situation with her now ex-husband. She was free as a bird to do whatever she wanted to do and Chaya was a little jealous by her friend's new found freedom.
    With tears in her eyes and what sounded like a frog in her throat, Chaya responded.
    "Well not really. I am just tired. I haven't been sleeping at night because you know when my kids need something and I don't see a way with my natural eyes, I continuously wreck my brain, stressing and wondering how? And I know better than to worry but it is hard not to. Chas' you and I both know that being a mother is a task and a half! One moment your kids are your pride and joy, and the next, you're wondering if you are cut out for this mothering thing?"
    "Well, whatever moment you fall in or out of, just know that you no longer have a choice as to whether or not you can continue your motherhood journey."

A. *Life* Gant

    Chaya's friend was now using reverse psychology on her because these were the very words she used when Chastity needed to hear them. For this reason, Chaya loved having a friend like her. Chastity continued.....

    "Time may or may not extend itself to be used, money can and will be used up, and love, especially for your children, can in no way be measured! You know who said those words, Miss Thang?"

    They both laughed as Chaya held back the tears that had begun to flow ever so rapidly.

    "Thanks Chas' I needed that. But you know what's so funny is that even in the smallest areas of my life as a mother and making decisions about the livelihood of my children's well-being, I still have the nerves to ask God what He is saying to me? And then I wonder if He's already spoken, did I miss what He said if He said anything at all? Chas' I just pray that I haven't missed Him. I certainly hope that I have not failed to listen or take heed."

    "Beep. Beep. Beep. Beep."

    "Chas' my other line is beeping. I will call you back later this evening, hopefully with happier news. Oh yeah and Chas'?

    "Huh?"

    "...Do something about your raggedy phone!"

    The ladies voices smiled and they both promised that they would re-connect later!

Chaya's First Death

Chapter Two

      Chaya was a quiet person and for the most part she kept to herself. Leaned against the sink and staring out of the kitchen window, her mind took a walk. Usually when she was alone with her thoughts, she would think back on her days as a child and wonder how her mother, with all the obstacles of life, managed to make it. And here she was on the verge of a breakdown.

~~~~~~~~~~~~~~

      "You all take me for granted."
      Words her mother used to say in so many ways, without exactly saying them.
      "Y'all fail to realize that although you have your physical needs met, you forget that I'm the one who takes care of them! You carry no responsibility at all but one day you will, when you get grown!"
      She wanted to call her Momma and talk to her, but she was at work, so she just kept her thoughts to herself.
      "Momma, you were right! Boy were you right! Now that I'm a big girl with two little girls, I completely understand what you meant when you said, we took you for granted. The catch is, it's not the little ones birthed from my womb, but the one whom I have begun to travel down life's road with. Although I am sure they too will have their chance to take a stab at this puzzle, my partner is the one, who at times causes my heart to skip beats, and I don't mean that in a good way!"
      Chaya laughed at the thoughts she was having with herself

A. *Life* Gant

and without reason, she said aloud:

"I am too young to die of a heart attack and I refuse to do so, for I have a 'lotta livin' to do!"

Those were the words of her late grandmother and she held them close to her heart.

"Man I sure do wish Mama was still around to give me some much needed advice. I just need her to tell me everything is going to be alright, like she used to. She too had to deal with a man who was very unstable financially. Oh well," Chaya thought.

She now had to do things her way. The way she felt was right.

~~~~~~~~~~~~~~

Later, that evening during dinner, she and her husband had some heated fellowship and since he hated confrontation, he just shut down and walked away while she was speaking.

"Why won't you say something?"

He was silent and Chaya was getting more upset by the minute.

"Hey man, I need help taking care of this house! The bills are over due and the phone never stops ringing because the creditors want their money! Can you blame them? Wouldn't you want to receive what's due you if you loaned or gave something of value to someone in hopes of a return? Wouldn't you Josh?"

Joshua was very stubborn and when he didn't want to talk, he kept quiet until he got good and ready to do so. Since he failed to respond, she continued.

"I'm tired of all the heartaches, the headaches, the disappointments, as well as the phone calls. I have never been in a position where everything is not only due but past due! What do you have to say about that? What do you have to say for yourself Mr. Goody two-shoes?"

Chaya's husband was assistant chaplain at his company and he made sure everybody knew it. He talked to everyone about everything. But when it came to his wife, Chaya, he barely had

Chaya's First Death

two words to say to her. Their relationship had pretty much gone down the drain over the last few years and neither person had the know how to fix it. The question remained whether they wanted to or not.

Chaya was never one to talk about what she'd done for her husband when it came to being the sole provider. His lack of sufficiency was not only painful to her but rather embarrassing. Now was the time she said something to him about her feelings. Only how would she say it? The way she was feeling, she could say anything and wouldn't care how much it hurt him. She just wanted, no, needed someone to hurt as bad as she was hurting. Chaya began to pray to herself and ask God to give her words that were sensitive enough to be heard, yet sharp enough to be felt!

~~~~~~~~~~~~~~

"Hey Josh, you got a minute? We still have to finish the conversation we started earlier. Are you ready to do this in a civilized manner, because you shutting down is not going to work? I believe you are taking me for granted. But I will let you start first. Where do you want to start?"

He grudgingly asked, "Chay' what do you want me to say? Since you know so much, no...since you know everything! Naw, I'ma let you start, Miss know-it-all!"

Chaya was about ready to burst at his last comments so she let him have it!

"Joshua, you fail to realize that when you lay down at night on a bed you didn't pay for, you take me for granted. When you wake up in the morning, flip on the light switch, and Aha!, you have light, you take me for granted. When you go to the restroom to relieve yourself and brush your teeth, both requiring at least cold water, you take me for granted. Want to take a hot shower? You take me for granted. Don't forget to stop by the kitchen and open up the fridge, 'Oh my gosh' food awaits! Not secretly hiding as to keep itself from being consumed, but sitting there patiently waiting to become pleasurable to you, to fill and

A. Life Gant

sustain your very being. Remember when you take hold of those items, you take me for granted!

Josh looked at his wife like she had gone completely crazy.

Chaya went smooth Off! By now, tears were akin to her caramel brown skin. She got up from her seat and walked towards the bathroom to get cleaned up. Looking in the mirror, Chaya questioned her reflection as if it would speak back.

"Why am I putting myself through this? And what is this thing that so seemingly has itself attached to me?"

The word Enabler kept coming to mind.

"Huh? Now Lord," she said to herself but directed it towards heaven;

"I am not up for any English lessons so just tell me what that word means or lead me to the dictionary that is probably hidden or stuck somewhere under something that is under something else! Uugh, uh, whew!"

Breathing like she had just run a marathon, Chaya searched high and low for her little pocket dictionary. She almost resorted to going to the store to buy another one but kept getting this feeling to look in a place where she had not.

"I found it!"

The red, worn out, school book was under her bed where she had left it when she was up late one night writing.

She screamed cheers of excitement as if she had just won a million dollars. In fact, she just may have. After this stage in her life was over, she knew that overcoming this generational curse would do just that.....cause God to bless her and her family through various avenues, with millions, to be able to help others in the same situations.

As Chaya began to straighten out the crumpled and dog-eared pages, this word kept bothering her. She kinda knew what it meant, but did she?

'Webster states: enable is to make possible, practical or

Chaya's First Death

easy; to provide the opportunity; to cause to operate.'

"Wow," she said with tears in her eyes.

"Lord, You mean to tell me that that is what I am doing?"

Chaya's tears became her meat night and day. At times she could be heard repeating that word.

"Enable." She would say softly.

For the next few days, Chaya would just perform life. Whatever she needed to do, she did it, but as a robot. Her children were still cared for but without the presence of 'their mother'.

The performance on her jobs didn't suffer either because they only required her to perform.

Life went on, but it didn't. She was sure no one would notice, but they did. They were just too coward to call her on it, she thought. Who is this woman that can look and act like Chaya but not be her? Where had her spirit gone? Her tenacity? Something had to be done about this situation so the real Chaya in her did what she knew to do...

"Dear Heavenly Father, First of all, I want to thank You. I want to thank You for what You've done. I want to thank You for what You're doing. But most of all, I want to thank You for what You're getting ready to do! You have Blessed me beyond measure. You have made ways out of no ways and for that...I want to thank You..."

Nothing could hold back her tears now because she was talking to her father, her Heavenly Father.

"...Lord You have called me to be the Head and not the tail, above only, and not beneath, the lender and certainly not the borrower, so for that I thank you!"

Chaya knew that when praises went up blessings came back down and that was her intention, to receive a blessing from God.

"Forgive me Lord, for getting in Your way. I have played God unknowingly. If there was a need, I tried to fix it! If something needed to be done or taken care of, I had my hands on

A. *Life* Gant

it! Forgive me God because that was not and is not my job. It's Yours! So I am giving it back to You!"

The strength He gave her begin to rise up and boldness came forth.

"I'm not doing it any more! I refuse to place my own wonderful self in positions to be taken for granted. I will not and can not allow myself to be used up to the point of death! I know it's pretty much all my fault. Yes, I take the credit for it."

If you were listening to her praying now, you wouldn't have been able to understand her. She was crying dry tears. Her wet ones were all on the inside of her throat.

"...And you know what Lord?"

She questioned Him as if He didn't know everything already. As if He had spoken to her, she began again, this time it was just a little talk with Jesus.

"The funny thing is that I came from being a user, as a child so to speak, to being used as an adult! Now isn't it amazing how regardless of situations and circumstances, there will always be a time of a shifting of the roles. A role reversal, if you will. So thank You God for showing me, because if You had not, I wouldn't know that being on either side of this fence is not Your will for my life, nor is it Your will for anyone! So...in closing,... Lord...I must again say...Thank You!"

Chaya got herself together. She was Clean! Hair done. Nails done too. You couldn't tell her anything! She looked good and she knew it! BUT...would this last? Would her exterior now be a reflection of her interior? Only God knew, but time would tell.

~~~~~~~~~~~~~~~

"Hey Coy and Beta? Come here."
"Yeeessss?"

They asked this as if they were fed up with their mother calling them. This was the first attention-getting attempt. Usually it took two to three screams before take-off.

Chaya's First Death

Chaya's attitude could take off alright, especially when she felt she wasn't being heard. This was one of her main problems with Josh. He played crazy and even he knew it.

"Are you guys ready to go? We have to go to the store to pick up some groceries for the next few weeks."

She should have gone last week but her finances didn't allow.

"Hold on girls, let me go and ask your daddy if there is something he wants me to pick up while I am out?"

Down the hall she went. She expected him to be watching one of his favorite t.v. shows when she entered the bedroom, and that is exactly what he was doing.

"Hey 'J', is there something you want me to pick up at the store?"

"Huh?"

There he goes playing crazy, like he didn't hear me. Chaya did a quick ten-count in her head and then repeated herself. He almost tried that game again but he could tell she was not having it.

"Oh yeah get me some...and...some..."

Dang!, she thought. If his list gets any longer we are going have to take his truck!

"Is that it?"

He nodded and she continued.

"Okay, I need about twenty more dollars because I don't think I will have enough money for all of that."

Joshua simply said, as if it was the right thing, "I don't have any money."

Chaya walked out of her bedroom and back to where her children were waiting. She knew that had she remained in the same room with her husband, a major argument about his money issues, would have erupted, for sure!

~~~~~~~~~~~~

"Mom, can we have our own cereal this time? You said

A. Life Gant

when you got some money we could pick our own."

    Coy was very smart and she remembered every promise that was made to her. She was a lot like Chaya as a girl.

    "That's fine, you and Beta just need to hurry up because this place is packed and I don't want to be stuck in a long line." Chaya didn't realize that she was speaking in a tone that was unnecessary but she really was talking to their father through them.

    "Momma? Are we done getting all the stuff on the list?"

    Chaya nodded.

    "Dang, you got all of our house stuff and daddy's stuff too?"

    "Bay' watch your mouth!"

    The last pea of the pod, little Beta, even recognized that there was some form of separation.

    "Yes, we have everything. Since you are paying for it with your money ma', how about you and Coy run and go get your daddy's favorite cookies while I wait in this line."

    The girls laughed at their mother's joke about them paying for the food, ran to get the merchandise and returned to find their mother counting out all the change she could find.

    Chaya didn't have enough money for all her items and she began to pick and choose what to leave behind.

    Assuming she wasn't going to be able to get their father's cookies, they asked could they go return them back to the shelf.

    At the time, all she could think of was to swap something. But what? She was embarrassed.

    "I can not believe this is happening to me. Hey girls give me those cookies and take these back."

    She replaced her sandwich crackers with his cookies.

    What was happening and why was she doing this to herself? She wasn't doing her daughters any justice either.

~~~~~~~~~~~~

Chaya's First Death

On the way home, Chaya silently sniffled, wondering would anybody ever love her the way she deserved to be loved? Would that person treat her as she'd treated them?

As she continued down her thought-filled path, she could hear the Lord remind her of a phrase she'd read before.

"Never make somebody a priority in your life when you remain an option in theirs."

Her nasal sounds became that of a wart hog every time He spoke to her.

She pressed the garage door opener clipped on her visor and pulled into the external room of her home. Chaya let her girls out of the car but she took her sweet time because she and the Lord were still talking. She began to ask God rhetorical questions.

"Lord why am I constantly doing the same thing over and over? Why am I constantly returning back to my state of allowance? I wonder and ask myself did You allow my allowance? If You did, why? Is it to better understand myself or others? Is it an exam, similar to that of a mid-term? I am asking You these questions Lord because most tests are not as long and they don't require you to know as much, but exams contain far more material and the lessons to be learned cover whole chapters and books, as well as tests taken in the past. Well whether it's a life lesson, a mid-termish exam, or shock therapy of role reversal, I may never know. Although I'm convinced it is a combination of the three, my grade of understanding could be held up if I fail to complete any aspect of what You are trying to teach me! Is this something that needs to be taught to me forever? If so, why? What are You trying to teach me? What is to be learned and how will I know when it is over and if I've passed?"

She would wait for Him to answer because He always did.

A. *Life* Gant

Chapter Three

"Ooh I need to wash! I can't even get through this wash room!"
Chaya had to make her way through the door that lead to the garage by pushing up against it. Clothes were behind it, but there was a trail of passage created by kicking the soiled garments out of the way. The bags of groceries felt like they weighed a ton, but she pressed on anyway. She barely made it in. Squeezing through both doors with all the food was next to impossible.
"Josh? Are you busy? Uuuh? Can I get a little help bringing in this stuff?
"Oh, I didn't know you were back yet."
Chaya couldn't believe her ears. Why was he lying? The opening of the garage door was loud enough for the next door neighbors to hear.
"What do you mean you didn't know we were back yet? Josh the sound of the garage door ain't loud enough for you to hear? You would hear it any other time!"
He looked at her crazy and walked off as if she weren't speaking, having the nerves to talk smart under his breath.
"What is it 'J'? Is there something you want to say to me? If so, don't keep it to yourself."
Her husband, yelled some obscenity, went in the bedroom and slammed the door.
Chaya was so fed up with his unresponsiveness and his lack of ability to control any situation in his life. She never

~29~

Chaya's First Death

wanted to fuss and fight with him. In fact, they hardly ever argued. Joshua wasn't an aggressive person either. She loved that about him but believed that there are some things you must be aggressive and persistent about. The family and their finances were among the few. Chaya's spirit was broken and she could no longer hold in the pain of her wounded soul.

After the groceries were put away, Chaya went into the bedroom to get changed. She had been in her work clothes all day. From the drawer, she pulled out her favorite pair of sweat pants and a matching t-shirt.

"Where are you going?"

Chaya remained silent and when she didn't respond to her husband's question he asked her again but this time he got louder than before.

"I asked you a question! I asked you where you were going?"

Since Joshua didn't pay any bills, Chaya didn't feel she owed him an explanation. He didn't know when to stop. Josh was relentless and badgering her must have been his assignment.

Putting on the last leg of her pants, and growing weary of her mate's comments, the wall on the dam broke...

"I've had it! I'm tired of being responsible for everything! For the last...No! Let me get it straight. From the beginning or our relationship until now, I have footed the majority if not all of the bill. Yes, actual utility bills are included, but I am referring to the bill of our relationship turned marriage! Whenever and wherever there was a need, I made sure it was met. If the kids are without, and their needs arose, they know who to come to."

"You know what? If this is how you want it fine with me! I'm sick and tired of you always talking about money. You act like I don't do nothing around here. You act like you are the only one who is working to pay bills. I pay bills just like you!"

As soon as he accelerated, he backed off and shifted gears towards shut-down mode.

A. *Life* Gant

"Excuse me, what did you say? You said you pay bills? What bills J', what bills? I have yet to see any bills marked paid, that you put any money on. So I ask you again, what bills?"

"Chay I gotta have gas in my car, I gotta pay bills."

He was in the mode and he actually felt as if gas in the car and a couple of dollars given was paying bills.

"Please don't start with that because you are not helping out around here financially. Sure you may be paying bills....no, debts that you have created somewhere else but you are not bringing anything home. I want to know where your money is going? And I don't want to hear that you have bills or you don't know again because that is getting old!"

Chaya tried her best to be cool about the situation, but it was difficult and since he had the nerve to question where she was going, she decided to go for a run. She already had the right outfit on. The sweat suit was loose enough to jog in she thought yet it fit just right for a bike ride. Getting the pant legs trapped on one of the pedals was not happening, she was not prepared for anything like that. This was a time of cooling off and she needed it.

~~~~~~~~~~~~~

The decision to run was a good one. She loved to exercise because it was her way to release frustration. Jogging six miles at the local track was the usual, so today she would increase her distance.

Chaya could not understand what had went wrong in her life. She knew that the past had made itself a home in the present, but why? Why was it so hard to get ahead and away from what she witnessed as a child? Of course! She needed to talk to her Father. She would ask him more specifically this time. Before, her requested information was not along the lines of why things happened but how they happened. God had some major explaining to do. She would take up her discussion with Him as soon as she returned home from her run.

Chaya's First Death

When she ran, she really didn't care much for thoughts pertaining to stress. This was her time. Her time to enjoy the breeze and take in the scenery. The trees and the birds in them amazed her. It was something to marvel at because when she was on the trail, she would always see one bird on a power line and it reminded her of herself. All by itself resting on something small enough to hold in hand yet big enough to give light to the world! *Wow God!* She marveled. *How great thou art!* Chaya had a newfound love and respect for the creations of the Creator and endeavored to be a better everything, beginning as soon as she returned home. She smiled and sang praises while on her last lap and didn't stop until she reached the doorsteps leading up to her house.

A. *Life* Gant

Chapter Four

The voice of gospel diva, Yalonda Adams blasted from the surround sound speakers. She was singing Chaya's favorite song, 'The Battle is not Yours'.

There was more than enough of her favorite bubble bath left and she poured it under the running bath water. She had drawn it so she could soak the pain away. The pain from her past, the pain of her present and the pain she felt in her aching muscles.

Yalonda was speaking through song what she needed to hear and the songstress was right.

"The battle is not mine, It doesn't belong to me!"

Chaya stepped into the hot water, toes first, and begin to drown her sadness in it. She was determined that with the washcloth she would wash away any and everything that caused her to bleed. Her failing marriage, the inability to love herself enough to let go and the needs of her daughters were the only issues at the moment that mentally plagued Chaya. The saline solution of life flowed from within and merged with its kin. This time, both ran rapidly down her face and committed suicide by jumping into the hot springs replica, the master bath's jacuzzi. She was consumed by the green liquid that turned into white foam as it came into contact with the inevitable. At first she thought she had put too much bubble bath in but quickly changed her mind.

"Good," she said to herself in response to the thought of someone barging in the door to interrupt her while bathing.

"That way I am covered and not exposed."

Chaya's First Death

Her thoughts must have been overheard telepathically. The girls were banging on the door wanting to be let in.

"Come in! What do you guys want and why are you all arguing?"

Her daughters looked at each other as if to convince the other to fess up the reason.

"Don't look at each other. Look at me and tell me the truth! I am trying to take a bath here and you all are acting like babies who can't sit alone for a few minutes. So tell me what is going on?"

Chaya was getting more tense by the minute. The girls were interrupting her "me" time and she was not happy about it.

Coy started in first.

"Momma, my pants are kinda too tight and my teacher said we need to bring some money for the honor roll trip and do you think we can go to Wal-mart and get some new underwear? All the ones we have now don't fit me anymore."

"Coy calm down and let's take care of one thing at a time. Now you are right about those pants. They are pretty tight, so go and change them."

Chaya closed her eyes and began to get back to resting in her bathtub.

"Um...Momma? What about the money for my trip at school and...?"

Coy made her mother remember that she had two other requests.

"Oh yeah Baby, Momma forgot. Uuh...I will give you the money before you go to school in the morning but you have to remind me, Okay? When I go to the store this weekend, I'll make sure I get you some pants that fit. And get both of you some new underwear because you've outgrown Beta. And sharing the same package is not an option anymore."

"Bay', what's up with you? What can I do for you ma'am, since you are standing there itching to say something?"

~34~

A. *Life* Gant

Beta was not small on words when she wanted something. "Weeelll...Momma, I waannted to knooow if..."

"Bay' spit it out and quit playing!" Chaya could get real irritated when Beta played around like that.

"Okay Momma, I want to know if you can buy me some new clothes too? Coy is getting some and I want some too."

"Beta, now you know I don't play that buying one something and not the other game don't you? Have I ever bought one of you something and didn't get something for the other one? Have I?"

"Nooo..."

She replied with an ounce of sadness and a gallon of cheer. She knew if she couldn't count on anyone else, she could count on her momma.

The baby girl skipped off but before she got too far, she remembered she had forgotten to close the bathroom door and just as her mother started to yell, she ran back to close it.

"Sorry momma."

Chaya's emotions were stirred up again and all she could do was weep. Quietly. She questioned herself.

"How could I as a mother, allow this to be so?"

She knew sitting back in a state of complacency was not even an acceptable option! Realizing that her finances were null and void, she resorted to doing what any real mother would do. The statement that would refer to her near-future actions was simply put as:

"Something is not going to get paid this month!"

Chaya was hurting deeply and she spoke aloud as if someone was in the room with her. Did she hear voices?

"What am I supposed to do? Allow my babies to go without? Should I make the girls wear boa-constrictor type clothing? Or better yet, go ahead an put slits in strategic places of their underwear, so the fit won't be as tight, which in turn the item would take on the very essence of a fruit roll-up? I think not! Or

Chaya's First Death

maybe, just maybe, the pants that have begun to quickly run away from their ankles toward their knees, we can rename capris? You have got to be kidding me!"

Although no human being was in her master bath with her, she knew the Lord was there listening and waiting to be her superman. If she would just let Him.

The mother of two, was about to embark on another journey towards husbandville.

Chaya hated asking her husband to do anything for her or the girls. She certainly didn't want to get into another argument over what even a blind man could see, needed to be done. Well at the risk of her children's needs going unmet for a season, she decided to hand the baton over to her husband and let him run the race for a while. She called for him to come downstairs. He was upstairs playing a video game against the computer and it was winning. She rehearsed what she would say to him when he came down. "The girls came to ask me for some much needed items and I told them I would take care of it. They need some new panties and some clothes because you know Coy is growing out of everything. And you have said yourself that her clothes are getting too tight. So what are we going to do? I don't have any money and your payday is coming this week." "Yeah that's what I will say," she thought. Only Chaya didn't know what lied ahead. She would not be prepared for what he would say to her about taking care of the needs of their children.

His much anticipated arrival was an unexpected storm.

"What's up Chay'? I was about to win before you interrupted my game!"

Josh knew he was lying and he acted like he came down as soon as she called him. He was still playing and in fact, he had beat the the thing! After he won and was advanced to the next level, it was then that he came down, and not a minute before.

"J', I am sure you overheard the girls request for some much needed items...."

A. *Life* Gant

She continued slightly down the path that she rehearsed earlier.

Joshua looked intently at his wife and admired her beauty and her strength. He knew that what she was saying was true and he wished he could be better and do better than what he was currently doing. He just didn't know how he would be able to tell her again that he had no money nor means to complete his life-long mission: to be a better husband, father, and man of God.

"J' are you listening to me? I am spilling my guts to you and I am doing it in a calm way. I am not yelling or going off but I feel the need to do so arising because you are looking at me like I am speaking a foreign language."

"Yes, baby. I hear you but I am just trying to figure out how I am supposed to do all this. You know I don't have any money and yet you keep asking me if I have some as if it is somehow going to magically appear."

Josh knew he should not have patronized her because that was an automatic 'go-off' button, needing not to be pushed.

Chaya started again, this time her tone slightly raised.

"J' how many times must I remind you that I need you to step up and take your place as husband first and father second? Don't you think it's your turn now? I have been in the game way too long and I am tired! Josh' you can not keep treating our lives as one of the video games you play! It's timeout for that! I believe I know what's going on but I want you to tell me so I can rest easy. Am I asking too much of you? If I am, tell me."

Her husband stood there and looked at her in silence.

"We have been married long enough for you to be open and honest with me. So tell me. What's really going on? Why haven't you helped me? There is no excuse in the world you could give me as to why you've allowed your wife and children to suffer and go in want, while you did what pleased you! I am not asking for a response that sounds good but I need you to come clean and do whatever you need to do to make our family, this team do what

Chaya's First Death

it needs to do to become winners. Winners at everything we as a family put our minds to do. Winners at life! So just keep in mind that from this day forward, I'm stepping aside. You can have it! The pain, the pressure, the heartache, as well as the headaches. To teach you that responsibility brings with it other visitors, who in turn become extended-stay guests! There is only one catch if that is what you want to call it. LOSING IS NOT AN OPTION, WE MUST WIN!"

His nods and half cracked smile meant that he understood and excepted the mission that was given to him.

But did he?

~~~~~~~~~~~~~~~

Sunday morning came and the air was filled with gospel music and a little bit of tension.

Chaya picked out her girls' church clothes and ironed them. While she smoothed out the wrinkles in each garment with the electrical appliance, she began a conversation with her husband.

"Hey, I've arranged for a payment extension on the electric bill and it will be due this Monday."

His reply was what you might have guessed would come from someone who lived where there wasn't a need for any electricity. A place where life could still go on without it.

"Oh well, it is just going to be cut off because I don't have any money!"

Chaya could not believe her ears and was on her way to 'go-off mountain'.

"What did you just say to me? I know you didn't say to me what I think you said and in that tone of voice!"

"You heard me."

"A normal man would say, "I'll see what I can do," or "If I can make some extra cash doing an odd job I'll take care of it," even though he knew he was lying. A real one knows that words like that may have softened the blow because at least they sounded good. How in hell, do you tell your wife of nearly ten years, something is going to be cut off because you ain't got nothing to do with that?" Chaya was mad and yelled at the top of her lungs to whoever might be listening because apparently Joshua wasn't. "Somebody? Anybody? Please, please, answer me! Lord, Jesus take me now! I need a vacation."

    Chaya took a mental vacation, physically! She had to literally remove her mental self from the situation via a mental block because she couldn't think straight and her physical being became conflicted with various types of illnesses. Her head constantly ached, her chest tightened on occasion, and her body did not respond to any of the medicine the doctor prescribed. Yet she went on as normal.

    At work she didn't get much done and that that she had, suffered because she kept staring at the clock wondering if the electric company dispatched one of it's workers to shut off service at her home. Chaya prayed for grace but really didn't expect to receive any because she was an advocate for the lender. Why not get paid for services rendered? Still she hoped for the best when she got home.

~~~~~~~~~~~~~

    "Momma, it's dark. What happened to the lights? Are they broke? How long are they going to be off? I can't seeee... I'm still hungry! I'm scared, me too!" Coy and Beta, her daughters, yelled. Both voices in sync.

    Chaya began to question her mental self. "How am I supposed to react and what am I supposed to say? Do I say babies I apologize for having to make you a sandwich, fix your pallet, and get you ready for bed by cell phone light, because it's your daddy's turn to be a man? Of course not!"

    She sure wanted to, just so her husband, their daddy, could feel the disappointment emanating from the girls when they found out this was something that could've been prevented. But she kept thinking what would her telling them that change? Definitely their

Chaya's First Death

attitude towards their father. Would that possibly make her look like the beacon of light? Whether it would or not, and whether she wanted to or not, that certainly was not an option!

Chaya was used to having the ball in her court and she had been playing alone for so long, that it became hard to pass it. She was afraid to and didn't know what was going to happen to the ball of her life if she passed it to her irresponsible, yet kind husband. So she refused to part with it. That's until the coach, God Almighty, came along and refreshed her memory on the fundamentals of team play. He instructed her again that the only time a player should be alone on at least half of the court, is on the free throw line when a technical foul is called. Yes you dribble and shoot alone, but after a while, even the weight of decision making becomes a burden and you must pass it. If not, you could find yourself in a position trying to be a one man or in this case, a one woman show and be taken out due to a mere injury, fatigue, and or exhaustion.

She marveled at the way God used the sport of basketball as an analogy to make her understand what was going on in her life. After all, Chaya did play basketball in school and it remained her favorite sport. She stopped interrupting what the Lord was saying to her and let Him continue. This time He spoke and it seemed as if His voice was audible. And since she was the intended recipient, only she could hear it.

"On the court of life, team play is in order and Chaya being a star player doesn't mean every quarter you're on the floor. Obviously, there's a reason for several players, and in your case, two. If I had not purposed it to be this way, when would you be able to call timeout? Chaya you are not indispensable and you can not take on several oppositions at once as you have been doing. A great player knows the value of his or her team. A weak one believes no one else can get the job done. That's how a codependent person or enabler thinks."

Tears began to flow down her face. God was right! She

A. *Life* Gant

was an enabler and she was working on that she thought. But a codependent? She knew Him to tell nothing but the truth because He was truth! Chaya began to talk to the Lord wondering if He was growing weary of her.

"Lord, I need your help. Codependancy to me is stronger than enabling, but help me change for the better. I recognize that my strength lies not in my ability to run this team I call my family, but in my willingness to step back and give someone else, in this case, my husband, a shot. The season has come for me to sit this one out and although I may not like it, it's for my own good. Besides, I am learning if I am all used up, what good will I be when my turn comes again? Lord help me allow myself to let go because I am very afraid. I don't want to have a turn in being the captain so often, but sometimes life happens. Just bless me to keep in mind, that regardless of how I feel, I must say to myself, "Self, Timeout! It's not your turn. You can't handle it all by yourself..."

She talked to the Lord and He gave her the answers she needed through her own prayer.

Chaya knew that when she stepped aside, her healing would begin. Yet she still feared that her mate would not take his new position serious enough to keep the family together.

Feeling her way through the dark house, she pulled the covers off of her bed and drug them to the living room. Chaya made a pallet for herself and her daughters in front of the fireplace. Because of there being no electricity, it was getting colder by the hour. Winter's arrival would be sooner than later. Nevertheless, she wrapped her daughters as tight as she could with her queen-sized blankets and tucked them in. The exchange was not a good one. Their throws barely covered her body but she layed down anyway and drifted off to sleep. She didn't expect to relive her childhood days in her dreams. But she would soon find out that this was a tactic God used to answer some of the many questions she had about her now adult life.

Chaya's First Death

<u>Chapter Five</u>

"You see them right there? This is Chaya and Daya, my daughters, and if you think about touching or even looking at one of 'em, I'll kill you!" Those words made her new manfriend shake his head. Momma had a way with words, and like grandma those who heard her listened as well. Chaya didn't know whether to be embarrassed or proud of her mother's bold declarations. What she did know is that brother man didn't even give them a second look. Not to say he was going to anyway. He didn't so much as touch them with a handshake but offered friendly hellos.

Chaya and her siblings were raised not to allow anyone to touch anything that concerned them as well as they not touch others and their belongings. Seeing a one hundred dollar bill alone on the street for example, was fine. It was the hundred dollar bill in a purse or wallet that was considered untouchable, because that meant it had an owner.

Mister was a nice guy and he tried his best to please Chaya. But she had an attitude. She never liked any of her mother's boyfriends. There were a few times when he would wear her down with gifts. A smile might come across her little pie face. A frown would quickly replace it. He wasn't her daddy and unlike Daya who befriended everybody, Chaya would not allow him to try and play that role either. Her mother liked him. She must have liked him a lot because he was the new live-in.

"Baby I was just thinking about what you said that day you introduced me to the girls." Mister laughed a little. "I cant believe

A. *Life* Gant

you'd think I would do something to your kids. I have sisters. I belong to a decent family and that is something frowned upon in our house as well. You kinda remind me of my mother. Only she was like that about her whole family. I couldn't even imagine hurting a child in any way. I know you know me better than that. Don't you?"

    Mister questioned her. And Dinah thought she laughed to herself, until a loud 'Hmmph' came out.

    "What was that about and what is that supposed to mean? Mister asked.

    "Well since you want to know, I don't trust nobody with my babies, except my mama, and not even she can love'em like I can, because I had'em. And that point you made about me being like your mama, she ain't got nothing on me because I will not only kill you and yo family but any and everybody that is connected to you! Hmmph! Try me!"

    Mr. cracked up and instead of replying to what she had just said, he decided against it and just figured he found one crazy lady, whose strength he admired a lot. He allowed his thoughts to run through his mind just as the two of them drifted off to sleep.

~~~~~~~~~~~~

    "Hurry up girl, we gotta go! I told you to use the bathroom earlier! Now you gone make me late!"

    Chaya quickly pulled up her pants, not remembering to wipe herself as she had been told repeatedly. Instead she used the tissue to clean her face so no one would know she had been crying.

    Daya was already in the truck playing with some toy she stole from her big sister's collection. As she made her way to the back seat, Chaya kept her head down. Feelings of anxiety and sadness engulfed her all at once and the tears began to flow once more. Her mind told her to get her face together but her heart felt the need to pour of itself all the feelings stored so the pain of everything would just go away. That is until she saw Daya with

Chaya's First Death

her doll.

    All hell broke loose in the back seat but it was silent because neither girl wanted momma to go off. Besides, hell had already broken loose up front, and it was getting hotter by the second.

    "How are you going to tell me where I can and can't go? The last time I checked, I was grown and I pay my own bills! When you start taking care of business and pay some bills at my house then maybe, just maybe, you can have something to say but until then, Zip it!"

    Mister gave momma a look like he wanted to jack her up but decided against it because he knew what would happen.

    Yesterday they got into it about God knows what. All I heard was cussing and fussing at first. Then stuff started falling and breaking. Momma didn't know I was in the house. The fight was on! I wanted to go in and rescue my momma but it sounded like she had it all under control.

    Fights of all sorts happened in an around our place of residence. The next door neighbors fought. People down the sidewalk did as well. Fists, brass knuckles, bottles, cans, shoes and whatever could be found, were utilized. If something needed to be settled, whoever was involved didn't use many words. They just had it out, like men or women. There was no need for any real deadly instruments because all that took place was good ole' fashioned butt-whoopings. That was only until guns were introduced as a means to an end, by the fearful who did not know how to talk or duke out their problems.

    "I wish you would hit me again!" Dinah yelled at the top of her lungs as if to alert all who were listening.

    "I didn't hit you, you hit me, I'm just trying to keep your crazy but from wigging out! So I blocked your swing and tapped you on accident. Am I not supposed to defend myself when somebody is trying to hit me? Girl you gots to be crazy!"

    I quietly headed for the door, realizing that Daya was the

smart one because she was always outside and didn't care if the sun wasn't shining. When I met up with her and her playmates we went to the park to swing and Daya motioned for me to come here.

"What Day...what do you want? Somebody is going to steal the swing again and I'ma miss my turn!"

"Just come on! I gotta show you something."
As always Chaya went along with her fearless, younger sister.

~~~~~~~~~~~~~~~

"POW, POW, BANG, BANG!", became unwarranted music or need I say, racket to my ears! We lived a step up from the ghetto, in a place called The Manor. Gun shots were the norm in that part of town, during my youth. As a matter of fact, I remember living in those apartments at two different stages of my life. A few toddler years and then again in my adolescent, preteen years. Or maybe we stayed for the combined time of both and for some reason, I chose to block out a huge section. I don't know but time would tell.

When the shots rang, my sister and I found ourselves in an unprecedented situation. Earlier, she'd found, not that it was lost, a distant neighbor's, backyard peach tree, and she was excited about the pleasure of free fruit! I guess because of our limited amount of income, the idea of having an unlimited supply of anything was just that...an idea!

"Ooooh, I'ma tell momma and you are going to get in trouble.

"Chay' you can't tell momma because I'ma tell her you was with me! If you don't say nothing, you can have some. Plus we are going to take'em home so we can eat'em after dinner."

Daya had a way with words and she could get her big sister to do just about anything. She was a mini image of Dinah.

After she jumped the fence, making sure not to leave any of the stolen merchandise, we ran as if greyhounds or a huge dog of some sort, were on our trails, barking and panting as if

Chaya's First Death

tonight's supper was in view! Just as our breaths were commencing to leave our youthful lungs, we mustered up enough strength to dart across the street in time to barely be missed by the screeching tires on the suspects getaway car!

"Huh hoo, huh hoo, huh hoo," repetitiously exhaled from our bodies as each breath replaced the last.

~~~~~~~~~~~~~~

"Lord noooo! Why Lord? Not my baby!"

Miss Tonya cried as she grasped at the bloody corpse of her common-law husband, Leon.

That scene was too close to home, well it was pretty much home, seeing that our doors faced each other and were only a couple of steps away, across the hall! We would never have to experience death in that way again and our lives from that day forward, just wasn't the same.

"Momma, I'm scared", we cried.

We didn't have the security of bullet-proof windows and sleeping on the floor became the norm, out of fear.

"Well sleep on the floor then!", she said, not because she thought a bullet would come through an upstairs apartment window, but because to us, it just felt safer there!

Whether on the floor or in the bed, my sister would always want to sleep with me and gosh she slept badly. Nevertheless, I let her. While she woke up well rested, I felt the complete opposite.

The sleeping arrangements went on for quite some time until we moved, and in the process of moving to many different locations...one stop was to...grandma's house.

A. *Life* Gant

Chapter Six

"Chaya! Bring me your dirty clothes so I can wash them!"
"Okay", I replied.
My granny loved to clean. We called her Mama, because at our birth she felt she were too young to be called grandma. She absolutely believed that cleanliness was certainly next to godliness and no one questioned her either.
"Is this all of 'em?"
"Yes ma'am."
"Okay, now go make sure you wash your hands because dinner is almost ready."
I can still smell the aroma of hot water cornbread, neck bones, and white beans, simmering on the stove. Mama could cook and she knew it too! Besides her own, she rarely ate anyone else's food. Kinda like, if it wasn't done right, or the way she thought is was supposed to be done, it had to be nasty.
Boy did she mess us up! To this day, I still don't eat everybody's cooking.
"Say your grace, eat all of your food before you get anything to drink, and keep your elbows off the table!"
Those rules of etiquette became commandments and were never to be forgotten!
Mama's house was a breath of fresh air. Next to my daddy, my granny, well mama, had me rotten.
At her house we didn't feel an ounce of fear at all. Maybe it was because she took life and everything with it head on and

Chaya's First Death

dared any opposition.

    Strength was her god-given robe and she wore it with pride. It takes strength to keep a home running that housed at least seven people day in and day out.

    Whatever mama needed me to do, I tried to do it. Whatever I was big and bad enough to do, I decided that I would be her little helper.

~~~~~~~~~~~~~

    I kicked the covers off of me because I got hot and the morning dawn was calling me. Making my way to bathroom was stop number one because as I told you, mama didn't play. Now the morning commandments were as follows:

    "Brush your teeth. Wash your face. And thank the Lord for waking you up this morning!"

    After my cleaning ritual, I made my way to the living room where my granny was drinking a cup of coffee and folding a load of clothes.

    "Good morning baby."

    "Good morning mama."

    "It is some rice and bacon in there, go to the table and I'll fix you some."

    Waking up early to be with my granny was something I lived for as a child during my periodic stays at her house. I couldn't imagine how my life would've turned out had it not been for her. She was my world and my rock! I hardly ever felt alone when I was with her except on certain days when I longed for the affection of my natural mother.

    "Mama when is my momma coming to get us?"

    This question was not an everyday one but it was on my mind daily. My natural mother left us at granny's so she could get some rest, I suppose. The only problem was that our stay at grandma's was always for unspecified amounts of time.

    "I don't know baby. But no matter what you will always have a place in this house because my house is your house. Baby

A. *Life* Gant

you just have to pray for your momma because right now she is doing what she wants to do and she's being selfish, worrying about herself. She forgot she has kids, but like I said, don't worry, everything is going to be alright. She is just going through something, but she will learn and everything is going to be alright."

The words of my grandmother always soothed me. She had a way with the use of them and when she spoke, all who were at ears distance listened and payed attention. By this time, the house was awake.

"I'm sick and tired of folk playing games with other people's money and lives. They don't realize that it is not only them who is getting hurt but the ones closest to them. Kids running around hear wondering when their momma is coming to get them and where she's at. What am I supposed to say? What am I supposed to tell them when they keep asking me questions about stuff like that? All I know is how to be the best I know to be. That is what I taught all my children and that is what I am going to teach you all! I may not be the best mother or grandmother out there but I da** sure ain't gone' let y'all go without. Only time will tell how I did but all I know is that when it is all said and done and y'all stand at my grave crying, it won't be because I didn't do my job! I just pray that when it's time for you all to cross that bridge, you will be able to do it, with your heads held high because that's what I expect!...

Now go in there and get some clothes on!" she said as she lit another cigarette and went back to washing.

While I got dressed, I pondered over mama's talk. I trusted everything that woman said. If she told me to jump off a bridge, I probably would've done it! Not because she was controlling or anything but because I believed her and usually her suggestions were brought on by experience. My granny could have told me to go and cook a thanksgiving dinner at the age of nine and I would have tried it knowing that she'd walk me through it every step of

Chaya's First Death

the way and if I listened, it would turn out just right.

~~~~~~~~~~~~

    Big Valley was coming on. I found my spot next to my granny. wherever she sat, and we watched it together. We listened intently to the conversations the cowboys had about the guys who wanted to date their sister, Audra, and laughed at the way the boys fought over what seemed like the town broad. My grandmother laughed herself to tears and then had me go and get her some tissue to wipe them! She did that with all our favorite shows and it was just fine with me. I still don't understand how The Price is Right had the same effect! Oh well, it didn't matter because I was with my granny and at least half the world evolved around her.

    I loved being with my grandmother and wanted to be with her permanently only that was not and option because soon it would be time to go home. Momma was coming! I was a little excited no doubt, but who wouldn't be? My mother was coming to pick me up and that was all that mattered but I was saddened by the thoughts of leaving the mama in my granny.

~~~~~~~~~~~~

    Chaya woke up in a cold sweat and thought of the dream she had just had. Was it a nightmare? She didn't think so but she felt that maybe it was just leading up to some much anticipated answers to questions she asked the Lord about why her life was going the way it was. She tried to go back to sleep using different techniques. Pulling the covers over her head was one option. Another was shutting her eyes and squeezing them tightly as if not to allow any light from the bathroom in. When neither of the two worked, she got up and went to the kitchen.

    Trying not to make any loud noises while getting the small kettle out from under the cabinet where the pots and pans were, she lifted the handle on the sink and filled it with water. Chaya hoped she didn't wake anyone up or even slightly disturb their sleep.

The kettle began to *whistle*.

"Oh no!" she said softly and hurriedly quieted the steaming pot.

Chaya pulled out a coffee cup and a tea bag. She carefully poured some of the scalding hot water into the cup, sat down to a party of tea for one and silently asked the Lord why she was having dreams of her past and how she'd got to where she was in life and in her marriage. Before she could finish her conversation, memories of the past began to flood her mind.

Chaya's First Death

<u>Chapter Seven</u>

"Poppa was a Rollin' stone...Wherever he laid his hat was his home...but when he died...!"
She smiled and realized that was one of the songs her granny listened to when she had her house parties.

"James go in there and get us some beer. Tammy you want one?"
Tammy nods in agreement at Delta's question while on her way to Lala Land in Drunkville. She couldn't hold her alcohol well. As a matter of fact, she couldn't hold water or a secret either!
James, my granny's boyfriend, returned with the beer.
"Here baby", he said to Delta, my grandmother. After he opened up hers and passed out two each to the other guests, he sat down to enjoy one himself.
Mama shot him a look because evidently he forgot that he didn't pay for the extra beer he was giving out. So instead of going off, she said,
"James would you and your generous self go to the store and pick up some more?"
He couldn't say no because he didn't wanna hear mama's mouth.
She watched him in anticipation to see if he was just gonna leave and use his own money or not. But just as always he'd bring Delta her purse. He gambled his earnings away before

he got paid and had to use his paycheck to pay back his debts.

"Here!" She said aloud. And on a small piece of paper, she had written down what she wanted him to bring back.

This was done in secret and though she considered her friends to be alright, they were all selfish and greedy and usually got drunk off her money.

James took the note and slipped it in the front pocket of his work shirt.

"Take Tommy with you!" Mama yelled.

She was speaking of Tammy's man who was just sitting there staring at her as if she were a piece of meat and because her and her girlfriends wanted some girl time to discuss their sorry a** men, as they liked to put it.

The two men left.

Tammy put on another record and as the static from the needle filled the room with slight silence, the trumpeted tunes of Al Green, bolted out from the speakers.

"Bump, Bump, Bump, Bump, Bummm...Bummm... Bummm...Love and Happiness...Makes you wanna do right..."

All the ladies chimed in.

"Well!"

"That's it! That's it!" Mama said. "Al know' he know's what he's talking about! Love is something though ain't it? You try your best to be good to them and they walk all over you. Sh** he taking my kindness for weakness." Delta was on her soap box while the other ladies sat in a drunken stupor. "I know y'all know what I'm talking about! These brothers need they a** whooped and I'm just the one to give it to them and do it with my good leg!"

After she said that, they all had a good laugh. Mama was still laughing at the thought alone. She couldn't help but think of how funny it would look if she tried to kick somebody with her good leg while placing the rest of her body weight on the leg that had been giving her problems for so many years now.

Chaya's First Death

After the ladies came to themselves and took turns relieving their beer-filled bladders, they went back into the den to listen to the Blues according to Mr. B.B. King.

"Now Sandra you and Tammy both know I'm right about them men trying to walk on you, because both of y'all had to deal with it and to tell you the truth, still dealing with it!"

All mama's friends did was nod when she got to going because they knew she was crazy, but for the most part, partially right!

"Delta, you right about it. But don't forget we All been there, done that. And some of us still there!" Tammy rebutted, as if reminding Delta that her man, James, was sorry too.

Sandra was growing very tired of their friend Tammy always being competitive with everybody, especially Delta and decided that she needed to be put in her place. Then, she flew off the handle. "Tam' shut your drunk butt up! You are over there repeating what Delta just said! You need to snap out of it and learn how to control the licka' and not let it control you! And furthermore, quit trying so da** hard to be like Delta and be yourself! That's what this is all about! Control yourself, chile' and watch out for your man Tommy because neither him nor you is innocent!" She stopped there just as she felt she'd gone far enough. All eyes were now on Miss Sandra because she'd said a mouthful and usually was the quiet one.

Tammy knew San' was right because as far back as she could remember, Delta was the pretty one and could've chosen any man she wanted. She had beautiful, wavy hair; smooth, dark-chocolate skin and body shaped like a coca-cola bottle. It just wasn't fair for Delta to possess all of those qualities and Tammy resented her for them. On top of the looks, her friend also had a great personality and everyone listened to her when she spoke because her presence commanded attention. And while Tam' was slightly thinner than Delta, she certainly was not as pretty and her hair was as coarse as an SOS scouring pad. The more she thought

A. *Life* Gant

of her friend, the more jealous she became figuring she had a leg up on Delta when it came to her choice in men. "Yeah at least Tommy's got a good job and he don't gamble his money all away like James. At least he do have some left over to pay bills at home, because I ain't having no man lay up in my bed and not contribute like Delta's doing. Ha!" She thought to herself. "Finally I can tell her that if she say something else to me! My man Tommy, is better than your man James! Yeah, that's what I'm going to say!"

Tammy was really over there in deep thought and Sandra called her name to get her attention to see why she was so quiet. When Tam' didn't respond, Sandra screamed her name, snapping her out if it. "You alright Tam'?" She asked in an apologetic way. "Because you know I was just talking too much don't you? And I'm sorry if I hurt your feelings!"

Neither of the women, including Sandra herself, believed that apology because they all knew it was the truth and a drunk person usually always speaks a sober mind!

Delta managed as always to find a way to bring happiness to the situation. She started singing along with B.B.King...while adding a little bit of her flavor. "Well I guess...The Thrill is Gone...The Thrill is Gone Awaaay...!"

The ladies laughed together once again and toasted to friendship because that's what they truly were. Friends. And nobody could say anything different!

Sandra got up and began to dance all by herself. The others looked at her and snickered a bit, thinking how much of a mess she looked, but she didn't care, she was enjoying herself and made the best of her own, manless situation! That was a sad song nobody sang. Her husband of nearly twenty-eight years, died of cancer of the liver, and she'd been a nut job ever since! "Come on y'all get up and dance with me. Y'all know sitting around is not my thang. And Del' you know that jack-leg you got need to move some before it gets stiff on you!" Sandra was having herself a

Chaya's First Death

party alone and she wanted her girlfriends to join her.

All three women were dancing now. Each of the ladies had a raised glass in one hand and a cigarette in the other. Only Delta was sitting in her wing-backed chair, swaying from side to side and took a long drag of her cigarette before she began speaking.

"You know I sure do thank the Lord for keeping me alive. I should've been dead a long time ago, but He spared my life for a reason. A reason I don't know yet but it must be a good one because this here leg, keep giving me the blues."

Tears started to flow as Delta began to mentally recall the accident she'd had almost eight years ago.

David, the man she was to marry, arranged for them to have a romantic evening at The Shak to celebrate their engagement. She hated going to The Shak, not because she didn't like the food or the atmosphere, they both were great, it was just the route you had to take to get there. The owners of the restaurant wanted it to be exotic in a remote area that had a romantic feeling to it. The customers would have to drive to the outskirts of town, under a bridge needing to be repaired, and over the 'Y' shaped train tracks that were frequently visited by transient-filled box cars.

Delta was not a fearful woman, in fact, she was completely opposite. But when it came to going to The Shak and on this particular day, she had a bad feeling about it and knew when she ignored her gut feelings, the very thing she dreaded, usually happened. Needless to say, Delta did not want to go and tried to convince David as well, but he wasn't hearing her. So with much persuasion, she agreed and prayed God's hedge of protection around her.

Delta remembered the night like it happened just days before. She had picked out a blue dress to wear, some brown leather sandals with straps that went up her legs, and a thin, f aux leather belt to match. Her jewelry box housed all of her

A. *Life* Gant

accessories and she knew exactly what she would put on to compliment her whole outfit...a wooden, beaded necklace, dangling earrings and a bangle bracelet set.

On the way to The Shak, Delta couldn't shake the eery feeling she possessed. But she kept on praying and believed that God would keep His promise, one that said He'd protect her!

The couple was almost there when a huge rock from above fell just before they passed under the bridge. The black, Ford Ltd. came to a screeching halt, making sure it was out of harm's way, all the while, Delta was still praying, but this time she prayed hard and loud enough for all to hear. David assured her it was just a piece of the old bridge and nothing to worry about, not knowing what lied ahead. He pressed the accelerator and sped as fast as he safely could, under the bridge. He of course didn't want anything hitting his precious car, so at the thought of another piece of flying concrete tumbling down, his foot became as lead. Before he slowed down, he decided since the tracks were up ahead, he'd dart across those too, so his new fiancée would shut up.

"*BOOM!!!*"

A sound that could be heard from miles away with vibrations of the impact felt almost as far.

Mama's screams were high-pitched and painful to the ears of the witnesses. But at least they alerted the bystanders that life, inside the car, remained. David was instantly killed by the collision with the unmanned box car. The Ford's driver's side door and it's driver was crushed towards the passenger, just at Delta's left side, her leg included.

By now, Tammy and Sandra were huddled around Delta sobbing uncontrollably as if they'd heard Mama's thoughts aloud.

"Hey y'all, I'm alright I was just thinking back on how good God's been to me. Even when I didn't deserve it! He keeps right on taking care of me and I know better than all of this.

She motioned at the empty beer cans and cigarette butt-filled ash trays. But I sure do thank Him for giving me another

Chaya's First Death

chance to tell somebody about His goodness, while I'm amongst the land of the livin'"

    The music was off now and the party was pretty much over when Delta and Tammy, as if they read each other's mind, said the same words at the same time...

    "Where are those men at?"

    James and Tommy had been gone a while and their women were starting to worry. So they put on another record. This time a '45 of Marvin Gaye's What's Goin' On? and started cleaning the place, picking up the crushed, beerless cans and emptying out the ashtrays, while they waited for the two men to come back from the store.

A. *Life* Gant

Chapter Eight

"James you are a lucky man to have someone like Delta. She got a good head on her shoulders. She is a hard worker and on top of all that she's fine as hell!"

Tommy stated some facts. But James didn't know whether or not to beam with pride or be upset about his friend's statements. So he just nodded in agreement with a slight smile on his face. Tommy continued.

"Naw man I'm as serious as a heart attack. She's got it going on and if I were you, I'd be careful to take care of business with that because any man would love to have her..."

James was getting irritated now because, one: this man kept complimenting his woman and two: he was putting him down about not taking care of business, on a sly. This time he broke in on his riding companion's little chat and exclaimed,

"Man, please! I know what I've got. And I know how to take care of what I've got. You just worry about yours, because I'm tired of hearing you talk about my lady in this fashion. What? You acting like you want a piece of her. Huh? You want her? You want Delta?"

Tommy grew quiet. Yes, he thought Delta was fine. And he did want her. But he knew better than to mess with his friend's woman. And even more so, his wife's best friend. He was raised better than that!

James was still goin' off.

"'Cause I dare any man to come upon my territory and try

Chaya's First Death

to take what's mine. I dare'em!"

Tommy just stared at James because he was now becoming irate! Apparently, his relationship with his woman and his manhood was threatened and he knew it! He knew he had a gambling problem. He knew he had money issues outside of the gambling problem. And he also knew that because of those two things, Delta, his woman, was considerably affected with the burden of having to be the sole provider, when in fact, that was his job! But even more so, he knew if he continued down the same road, Delta was leaving him and who would want him then? Where would he go?

~~~~~~~~~~~~~~

"Ding, dong, ding!"

The bell on the convenient store door chimed, alerting the clerk that a customer was present.

"Hey man. Where are the big cases of Budweiser? You know uh...the 24packs? Because you out of them in the fridge?" James questioned.

"Uuh...let me go and see if we got some in the back."

The clerk responded and left towards the back of the store.

"Tommy, so what's been up with you? How's the business of taking care of other's people's money?"

James hardly ever asked about his being a banker so he welcomed the questions, while James continued.

"I'm sure it's good because you and Tammy look like y'all got it made in the shade. Tammy try to keep herself up by frequently getting them ole' Jheri curls on her head and you keep your's fried, dyed, and laid to the side."

Both men cracked smiles.

"Plus, y'all dress real nice."

Tommy couldn't help but laugh at James' observations of Tammy's hair, while thinking about what she really looked like when her curl need to be retouched.

"Yeah man, it's pretty good, but you know it's still a job

A. *Life* Gant

and I got to clock in like everybody else. I'm just glad they started what's called *celery* pay. I think that's what they call it. But anyway, it's where you get paid a set amount for the year no matter how many hours you put in. But it can be a good and a bad thing. You can work your forty and be good, or you may also work sixty but still get paid for twenty hours less. Either way, it pretty much evens out. So to answer your question again man, I guess I'm doing pretty da** good and to keep a decent job nowadays is kinda rough."

"I hear you." James said to Tommy in response to the answer of his question.

While the two buddies were conversing and waiting on the clerk to return with the case of beer, the store's door bell rang again.

This time, three guys entered with long black trench coats. Tommy nodded, as if to say hello, and James was still speaking with his back towards the door, so he didn't see the visitors. Each man went down separate aisles, simultaneously.

Finally, the teenage, male clerk emerged from the stock room with the last case of Budweiser, King of Beers. James was pleased because this was Delta's favorite and she wouldn't drink any other kind. As he pulled out the money from the pocket on his shirt to pay for the merchandise, one of the three guys came up behind him with a gun, shushing Tommy and the clerk, and put an arm around James' neck.

The clerk and his two regular customers, were being held up...they thought!

"Didn't I tell you I wanted my money yesterday? You told me you got paid Friday, well today is Saturday! Where's my cash?"

"Man, I-I said I get paid next Friday. I-I'll have your money, I swear, I swear, I'll have your money!", James said repeatedly with tears in his eyes.

Chaya's First Death

He tried his best not to let one drop because he didn't want to look like a punk in front of his friend Tommy. But by now, it was too late! The loan shark's grip was getting tighter by the nanosecond and James wanted to appease him quickly in hopes of a release.

Viewing the twenty dollar bill James had in his hand, still held in mid-air, Tony, the loan shark, blurted out...

"I thought you said you didn't have my money. How are you paying for this here beer?"

" I-I don't have no money....this is my woman's money and she's the one who sent me to the store!"

"Yeah right! I should take it so you can have hell at home too, but I'll let it slide this time cause I'm doubling what you owe me anyway!"

Tommy stood close enough to the situation to view the small beads of sweat on his friend's forehead begin to mix with the tears that became a steady stream. However, he couldn't move to help because guns were pulled on him and the clerk, but that didn't stop Tommy from voicing his opinions.

"Hey man, do you have to do this now? Can you just let go of the brother? He said he gets paid next Friday and he can pay you then!"

"Shut yo' punk a** up! You ain't got nothing to do with this! Unless...you wanna pay his debts for him?"

"Naw man, you right, I ain't got nothing to do with this but he is my ride home and right now that's where I want to be!"

The button that alerted the police was broken years ago and the tape that held it together was pretty much fused with the plastic. The threaded fibers that gave the gray duct tape it's character, were visible. Since this was the case and because guns were drawn, there was no need to try and see if by chance the button would work, one last time.

Now the clerk had begun to do as his grandmother had

A. *Life* Gant

taught him to do...Pray! Because he was a rebellious teenager and didn't pay much attention in bible class, all he could remember was *The Lord's Prayer* and that is what he began to recite, to himself.

His g-momma used to tell him...

"Let the devil hear you when you pray 'cause that 'ole devil need to know you got help coming!"

So he prayed aloud.

"Our father, who art in heaven, ...hallowed be thy name, thy kingdom come..."

He couldn't remember the rest but he'd felt he got God's attention anyway.

The young man forgot the ending but Tommy didn't and finished it up.

"...Thy will be done on earth, as it is in heaven. Give us this day..."

"Won't y'all shut up with all that praying because not even God can get you 'outta this one!"

Both fellows silently finished the prayer, but this time, only their lips moved.

"James, you got 'til Friday at seven pm! Not seven o' one, but s-e-v-e-n pee...em, to have my money and if you don't...OOH! You are going to wish you had. Because I'm coming to get it, in any shape or form....your car, for scraps and maybe even your life...naw' I'm going to let you guess what's gone happen if you ain't got my money!"

Just then, a light bulb came on in Tommy's head.

That's how they'd found them. Especially if James was trying to hide from his problems. He knew he should have driven his own car instead of riding with James in his beat up old '76 pick-up, but James insisted! Who wouldn't be able to recognize that thing? It was supposed to be a caramel-brown color but it was far from that. It had dents and dings all over it from James' line of

Chaya's First Death

work at the plant, and they became rusty. So it was part brown, part orange, from the rust, and of course you can't forget that blue hood from the savage yard that replaced the old one and not to mention that pastel green door he took off his old truck was now the driver's side door! Oh my gosh, he thought, of course, a blind man could spot that truck a mile away!

"Did you hear what I said?"

James who was now trying to control his asthmatic breathing, slightly shook his head in agreements as the last tear fell down his cheek.

"Alright...Friday! And I won't be so nice next time!"

Tony finally loosened his choke hold grip and snapped his fingers, signaling his entourage that the job was over and they were free to leave.

James dropped to his knees in exhaustion and held his throat, gently rubbing the painful wrings away.

"Man y'all I am sorry. I apologize. I didn't know they were coming because I told him I got paid next Friday! I swear I did! But I'm so sorry for getting y'all mixed up in my mess! And to think he was gone take Delta's money and beer! I would've been in worse trouble when I got home!"

He let out a fake laugh and so did the others at the thought of Delta beating him with her cane!

However, because of the day's events and because he knew he was traveling down the same road as his senior customer, the clerk felt if he continued down his current road, he would die young. He was ready for a change and a new beginning.

"I quit!"

He'd called the manager and told him to get there as soon as possible because tonight was it for him! He was moving back home to his G-momma's and going to church tomorrow to give his life to Christ again and this time it would be for real!

There was no need to call the cops now because nothing was stolen and all, including people, was accounted for.

A. *Life* Gant

    The ride home was not quiet by any means. Tommy yelled at James about how he needed to chill out with all the gambling and stuff and James agreed. He still couldn't believe what had just happened and couldn't help but wonder, when he got home, what was he going to tell Delta?

Chaya's First Death

Chapter Nine

"Y'all ready?" Momma asked.

She'd come to pick us up from over granny's house. We'd been there, this time, over three months and almost thought we were there on a permanent basis!

"Momma where you been at? We missed you!"

Chaya questioned her mother repeatedly but momma didn't answer.

Just as Chaya began her interrogation process again, Daya came into the house, after Delta called for her, and ran quickly to her mother.

"Mommmma!"...and jumped into Dinah's arms. "Momma, I missed you, I'm so glad you came back for me!" Daya loved the very ground her mother walked on. Even if she saw her, during this stage of her life, in sporadic proportions.

Dinah kissed her children hello and her mother, Delta, goodbye.

"Come on y'all let's go. The cab is outside waiting."

Chaya and her little sister grabbed with their tiny hands, what little they could. Dinah and Daya headed for the door but Chaya ran towards her grandmother instead.

"Mama, I love you and I wish I could stay with you, but I know you need your rest too like momma did. Bye mama, I love you."

"Chaya, I love you too."

Chaya left the grasp of her granny and sadly walked to the

A. *Life* Gant

door where her mother and sister stood awaiting.

"Dinah how long? How long is this going to last? How long are you going to keep running around here like you've been doing? Dropping these kids off and leaving them here while you do what you want to do?"

Dinah brushed off her mother's question-filled speech and with an attitude spoke back.

"Mama I ain't got time for this! My kids ain't got to ever come back over here. Especially if I've got to keep hearing you go off on me!"

Delta broke in.

"Now hold on a minute, Dinah Marie! I know you ain't raising your voice at me! Have you forgotten who it is you are talking to?"

The cab had driven off and Dinah had to stop and listen when what she really wanted to do was jump in the cab and go. But she couldn't now! It was too late!

"You must be outside of your mind! If I've told you once, I've told you a thousand times, I brought you in this world and I can da** sure take you out! You know good and well I raised you better than this, with your disrespectful a**! All I've done was try and help you and this is the thanks I get? Dinah I already have one of your kids."

The other child mama spoke of was my big brother, Daniel. My granny had him pretty much from birth, so he definitely wasn't going anywhere.

"And I'm tired Dinah. I'm tired of taking care of other people's responsibilities. I'm through raising kids, because I have already raised mine and now it's time you raise yours! I'm too old for this sh#@!"

Dinah was crushed. How could her mother say such things? Had she forgotten that her eldest daughter was going through some stuff right now and just needed a little bit of help?

Chaya's First Death

Dinah thought to herself because she knew better than to disrespect her mother.

"Had mama forgotten that although she had my kids, I was at least sending some food stamps to help out? I love my kids and I would do anything for them, but dang I just needed and still need a little more time!"

Dinah stopped her thought process because she now had to find them a way home.

"Chaya, go in there and get me the phone so I can call your Daddy to come pick us up!"

Chaya yelled, "Yaaaaay! Daddy! Daddy!"

Her daddy was just that...her daddy. He could steal, kill, and destroy whatever and she would see no wrong. He treated her like a princess and she adored him for it. Whatever her little heart desired, if she asked him, he would get it for her. This was her daddy and she was daddy's pooh bear, his baby. Daya and her father didn't get along well because he said Daya acted too much like her mother Dinah, which was true.

Dinah avoided Delta at all costs.

"Chaya go put this phone back up! Your daddy said he'll be here in a minute." From daddy, that minute meant whenever he got free from doing whatever he was doing. But nevertheless, we waited anyway.

"Chaya go get momma the phone one more time."

By now, Chaya grew tired of being her mother's gopher. Dinah could've gotten off her butt to get the phone but she didn't want another run in with her mother.

"Here momma."

"Thank you."

"Five-five-five, zero-zero-seven seven", the phone was old and ragged, probably from grandma throwing it at James, but the volume still worked loud and clear!

"Hello?" A voice said on the other end.

"Hey girl, what you doin'?"

~*68*~

A. *Life* Gant

"Nothing."

Dinah called her good friend Sadie and when those two got on the phone, everybody knew it. They would talk for hours on end.

"What's wrong with you? You sound like you mad at somebody."

To get some privacy, Dinah walked outside and sat on the front porch. The curly fry-shaped cord, stretched throughout the entire house, so nobody questioned if it would make it outdoors.

"Sadie, I'm so tired of this sh-stuff."

She wanted to say something else but she knew better. Delta did not allow anyone but herself, especially not her children, to curse or say anything out of the way for that matter.

"Mama in there trippin' about the usual."

"Did she say anything about what time you came to pick up the kids? 'Cause you know you got pretty tore up last night and I'm surprised you woke up at all!"

"Shut up Sadie with your crazy butt, I mean self. You were worse than I was! Anyway girl, where's your kids?"

"They around here somewhere."

Sadie lied. In fact, she didn't know where they were. She left hers at home alone on a frequent basis and anything could have happened. The State could have had them or her mother, who was just as worse as the state. She and Dinah were the best of friends, but when it came to the welfare of their children, they differed greatly. At least Dinah's mother Delta would take her grandchildren in, but not with out a word. On the other hand, Sadie's folks were crazy. They were liable to take her kids and not even call her with their whereabouts.

Dinah always told her they were too young to be by themselves, but Sadie would always ask what her option were. She had no one. The two women almost fell out over the issue of Sadie leaving her children alone at home, somehow Sadie always found her way around everything by lying, which would soon

~*69*~

Chaya's First Death

catch up with her.

"Anyway girlfriend, who was that you were talking to at the bar?" She questioned Dinah. "He sure was good-looking. Did he offer to buy you a drink and ask you to dance?"

"Dang Say' you are nosey!" She laughed. "To answer your question, I don't remember his name, he was fine, and he did buy me my favorite drink, a long island iced tea. Afterwards, I danced with him but he couldn't hang!"

"Ha ha ha, girl you are crazy! Dee," as she liked to call her, "not everybody can dance like you. That's why when you get to doing all that screaming and yelling, I sit down, 'cause not even I can hang with you. Dee, you are in a league all by yourself!"

The two friends were laughing because they knew that was right. Dinah was a dancing machine and when she danced, a crowd of people would gather around her to cheer her on.

"Say' shut up!" she said jokingly. "Let me finish telling you about TDH."

"Who?"

"Girl that's my acronym for tall, dark, and handsome!"

"Oh. Okay, I'm listening."

"Well, TDH, was all upon me trying to grab on me. You know I had to go off because I don't play that! But anyway, he told me he had two kids, a girl and a boy, and they live outta' state with their mother. He also said that he and his mother were living together so he could help her out and that right now he was between jobs! I 'bout choked on the last swallow of my drink when he said that! Two words Say'."

"MOMMA's BOY!"

They both blurted out and laughed at the same time.

"I couldn't talk to him any longer. Sadie now you know I wanted to hurt his feelings but I left him alone and danced into the crowd until I lost him!"

"What happened then girl?" Sadie asked.

"I'm getting to that, hold your horses! So as I was saying,

A. *Life* Gant

TDH, who I'll now call BDH, for broke, dark and handsome, was looking all around and I could see him twisting and turning to see where I was. I cracked up and then all of a sudden...Mister grabbed my arm!"

"What?!"

"Girl yes! He grabbed me from behind so I didn't see him. Before I realized who it was, I tried to jerk away, but the grip got tighter. He shooshed me and I almost went off until he introduced himself."

~~~~~~~~~~~~~

"Ooh boy you was getting ready to be a dead son- of- a-!"

"Watch yo' mouth", he said as he smiled and released my arm. "I thought I told you not to come here any more?"

Dinah looked at him like his face was a dirty diaper and rebutted.

"The last time I checked, your name wasn't on my birth certificate and not even he can tell me what to do. He may make some suggestions but I'm legally past twenty-one, therefore, I RUN THIS!"

She air caressed her body.

All Mister could do was laugh at her because this was one little feisty lady, as he'd put it!

"No, for real Dee, I don't want anybody else checking you out or even getting a chance to rub against you while you are dancing, so promise me you wont come here no more!"

If looks could kill, mister would have been pulverized!

"Like I said, I run this, not you, and how do you think you can tell me not to do something when, in fact, you are doing the same thing? Man, you must be trippin'!"

Mister tuned her out and just stared at her. She looked like she was in super slow mode. Her lips were moving and so was her neck. One hand was on her hip and the other was snapping its fingers mid-air.

"Look at her", he thought. "How could a woman this fine,

Chaya's First Death

be so da** mean? She was the whole package with the exception of a few flaws in the attitude and mouth department. Her body had the shape of a larger scaled hour glass. She had a little bit more than enough of everything a man could ever want, in all the right places.

As he was beginning to return from dream land, her body movements were beginning to speed back up to reality and her big, bouncy, wavy, almost afro, was commencing to fall flat. Dinah's hair was a lot like Delta's. It was beautiful. It didn't get kinky or extremely tight like most because they were part Indian. Her scarf kept creeping backwards the more her neck popped. It had acted as a headband at first, but now it was almost in a ponytail.

"Did you hear what I said? You are over there just skinning and grinning like I have not said one word!"

Just as Mister was about to respond, some lady motioned for him to come there.

"Dee, hold that thought" he said, made his way through the crowd towards her and they left the club... TOGETHER!

~~~~~~~~~~~~~~~

"Dee, you are lying! Please tell me you are not serious. Are you serious? I know you went off. Well I guess you couldn't , because he left, but are you serious?"

"Yes Say' I am extremely   S-E-R-I-O-U-S! That no good for nothin'..."

Chaya interrupted her mother just as she was getting to the good part of letting Mister have it.

"Momma? Mama wants to know if you are hungry because she fixed some spaghetti and chicken?"

"Yeah, I'll get some la...No. Tell her I'll be in there in a minute."

Chaya left to relay the message to her grandmother but there was no need because she had heard every word and for that matter, she'd heard her entire conversation.

A. *Life* Gant

Delta went to the front door and cracked it just enough to speak without letting flies in.

"What's this about you will be here in a minute?"

Delta was ready to let Dinah have it again!

"Sadie, I'll talk to you later, when I GET HOME!"
She added the last words of her sentence with an attitude.

"You keep on with me and you won't be alive to make it home! Now Dinah Marie, you know that when I cook, everybody in this house, eat at the same time! 'Cause afterwards the kitchen will be closed and there will not be any running in and out of my ice box!"

"Okay Mama".

"Don't "okay Mama" me. You are just saying that to get me to shut up!"

Dinah laughed within herself because she knew her mother was right. But how'd she know?

"No really Mama, I mean I am listening to what you are saying."

"Hmmph, that better be the lie you tell!"

Delta began. Momma chose a bowl from the cabinet and a fork from the silverware drawer. As she fixed her plate, granny was already on a roll with the kids and all.

"Don't waste nothing on my carpet and..."

"Had granny forgotten she gave us some newspaper to put under our plates?" Chaya thought.

Dinah tuned her out because all Mama did the older she had gotten, was fuss. To stay out of her mother's way she decided to eat at the table in the kitchen.

"Chaya go in there and get me some salt."

"Yes ma'am."

When Chaya returned with the salt, she and her sister were ordered to switch places with their mother.

"Dinah, come in here and let the kids have the table. Besides, I've got some more talking to do."

Chaya's First Death

Dinah reluctantly agreed.

"Now what's this I hear about some man grabbing your arm?"

Mama knew she was dipping when she came in the front room under the false pretense of watching television.

"What are you talking about Mama"?

"Now Dinah I know you are not going to sit there and play stupid! You know da** well what I'm talking about! I know you are grown and all, but I am just here to help make sure you don't go down the same road I went down.!"

In her mind, Dinah wanted to ask her mother, when she had gotten off that road, because by the looks of it, she was still there with James.

"Now you can do what you want but you are worth more than being used by a man and sure enough worth more than getting hit on by one! I've done a lot of stuff in my life that I am not proud of, that's why I keep on to you, so you don't travel down that same road. I've been through the pushing and the shoving matches with your daddy and you see we ain't together don't you? 'Cause nobody, not man, nor woman, deserve to be hit or beat on!"

Dinah's feathers were slightly ruffled when it came to any negative talk about her father, she certainly was a daddy's girl. That's why she couldn't say anything about Chaya and her love for her father, because she understood.

"Now you can take it for what it's worth, or not at all, but don't let no man hit on you or use you, because you are worth more than that, you hear me?"

Dinah nodded in agreement, sat and wondered when her children's father was coming?

Chapter Ten

"Good morning, baby."

James rolled over to kiss Delta and she moved away from him because she was ticked about him taking so long at the store the other night. James thought he was out of the woods when she didn't say anything that night but he was stupid to even think Delta would not remember.

"Okay, you can start talking now. I am sober and I'm listening. I want to know where the hell you and Tommy were the other night and what took you so long to get back?"

"Well, baby you know how we keep talking about my getting my stuff together with the gambling thing? Well, just so you know I had a wake up call and Tommy and I talked about my needing to change. It is easier to talk to a man baby, so that's what I did."

James was trying to get around to telling everything but the truth! He couldn't muster up the guts or the strength to tell Delta that he owed what he owed and that it was due in two days. How could he?

"James, now don't go telling me you had a *Come- to-Jesus* meeting with Tommy, because I know you are lying! I am just so sick of all this gambling stuff! You act like I am stuck on stupid or something! I have been putting up with your mess for way too long. I do what I have to do to take care of business on my end and I am still waiting on your part to come in. When is it going to stop James? When? Don't tell me you trying or that it is already

Chaya's First Death

stopped because that's a lie too! I want, no I need a date, as to when you will be completely through! When will all your debts be paid back and done away with?..."

James was getting ready to answer but Delta kept going. It was due time that she had a chance to get this weight off her chest because it had been there much too long.

"I have been paying all the bills and taking care of My kids by myself this long and I am well prepared to keep doing it. What am I supposed to do James? Am I supposed to keep letting you lay up in my bed and sleep with me without you helping me take care of business? Hell Naw! James you go to work and I know what you are supposed to bring home so you tell me what's going on? Yeah, we have already established the fact that you have a gambling problem but I know you ain't lost all your mind to gamble your whole check away! So, is this where you tell me you got another woman and you've been giving her money? I need to know! 'Cause I was a fool before and I ain't going to be one again. So I will give you one last time to come clean and tell me the truth about what's going on, where you were the other night, and where the hell your money is going!"

She was so upset that she started to cry. He didn't know what to say nor did he think she was going to take it like this. It was about time for her to say something anyway. She had only been hinting around a little bit but never really said anything right out.

"Baby, first I want to say that I am sorry for taking you through hell these last few months. I have had a gambling problem since we met, but never this bad..."

James tried to almost say that this was something she knew when they met at the casino, but he knew better.

"...I know that playing around with you and your feelings ain't right either. So just hear me out on this and please let me finish before you bust in. And if you let me explain everything I can promise you it would be easier that way for the both of us."

A. *Life* Gant

He sighed.

"Whew! Where do I start? Okay."

He composed himself.

"Remember when I told you that I bet on the horse race and lost? Well...that is not the only race I bet on. I put money on the football game too. So now, since I lost both bets I have to pay more out and thank God they gave me an extension."

James was now lying and although she could kinda tell, she let him continue his story and hang his own self. What she couldn't help but wonder was where and when he got the nerve to even use God's name in vain.

"Baby, when I get paid this Friday, I am going to take care of all the folks I owe. I am just tired of never having any money. That is the reason why I gamble in the first place. I have done it for so long and am usually pretty good at it. I mean, I can usually win some or at least break even, but lately, I have had bad luck and it has lasted too freakin' long!"

Delta could not believe what she was hearing. This man had the nerve to blame the mess he had created, on bad luck! Either way, she just couldn't shake the feeling she was getting about this whole thing. Again, Delta tried her best to avoid the reality that something wasn't right. Still, she buckled down and continued to listen to the madness her boyfriend, James, was talking.

"I think after this..."

He saw her face tune up.

"I mean, I know, after this season of bad luck, I may never gamble again. It would be good though to win a big one and go out the right way!"

The smirk on his face and the words he spoke, caused her stomach to do flips as if it were on a roller coaster.

"James, you better not say another word because I can't take any more of your lying. You've lied to me. You've lied to yourself. Hell James, you walk around living a lie. I gave you a

~77~

Chaya's First Death

chance to tell me the truth and you didn't. You gave me some half-a**ed story about bad luck and how you are tired of not having any money. Shoot, do you even realize who it is you are talking to? I have to pay every single bill up in here and do you think I don't get tired of being broke? My kids need things and who else can they depend on? Certainly not their no good-for nothing daddy! To tell you the truth, when I met you, my luck, since that is what you want to call it, has been nothing but bad."

Delta walked off.

He was heartbroken, but he knew she wasn't lying.

When he met Delta, she appeared to have it all together and she did. She had a house, a car she hardly ever drives, well-groomed children, and a job cleaning houses. Her home was immaculate. Her car was not new but decent. Her children were all either grown or almost grown, she just had her grandchildren a lot. For the last fifteen years, she cleaned the same houses and her bosses and boss' children, took good care of her. They paid her good money and if she ever needed help, they were there for her. Christmas was always a pleasure for her kids because at least one boss, would take care of the entire list.

So what James really thought, well, what he now knew, was that Delta was better off without him.

He brought nothing to the table and since this conversation was not accomplishing anything, he felt it was time to come clean. Now was the time for him to tell his woman what really happened and what was really going on. Maybe just maybe, his truthfulness would grant him his heart's desire, to stay with this 'good thing'. All he had to do now was pray that God would forgive him and in doing so, give Delta a forgiving heart as well.

James decided that he would give this praying thing a try. Both his grandmother and mother were praying women. Delta prayed quite often too. He remembered that she prayed daily as a matter of fact.

She would always say something like "Thank you Lord,

A. *Life* Gant

for looking beyond my faults and seeing my needs'".

Yeah that was it! He would say that to the Lord. God obviously payed some attention to her when she talked to Him because afterwards, she always said she would feel better.

On the other hand, did He really listen to her requests? She also asked the Lord to remove the desire to smoke cigarettes and drink alcohol away from her, but that hadn't happened yet. Maybe it is a process for some and miraculously instant, as grandma put it, for others? Either way, he felt he should give it a shot. So he knelt down on his knees, for the first time in...who knows how long...to pray.

"Dear God, I have not prayed to You in quite a long time. Probably since I was a boy. And I heard God, from my grandmother, my mother, and now Delta, that praying is just talking to God. So Lord that is what I'm going to do. I'ma talk to you. Now I do remember that You see and know EVERYTHING. You know about all of my problems. Could you please Lord, help me get myself together? I am tired of the way I've been living. I'm tired of feeling like I'm happy even when I am sad. I don't like going to work to make a living, only to turn around and put it in my 'holey pocket..."

Just then, he felt like something was happening. Was that a scripture from the bible he had read before or heard preached in the past? He didn't know, but it felt good. All of a sudden, James could pray a little better and because he now felt and prayed better, he unknowingly, got loud.

"Lord, I thank You for what You've done for me. You have taken care of my family, we'll my almost family, when I couldn't. I just want, no I need for You to do as Delta says, You can do. I need You to look beyond, and in my case even further, than my fauts' and see my need..."

"My need..." he thought.

"My need Lord, God is to get it right this time. My need is

Chaya's First Death

to quit all this gambling stuff and ..."

Tears began to flow and James began to cry out to the Lord like never before.

"...And all this lying, cheating, and stealing!..."

He was wailing by this time.

"Lord, I don't know what else to say but I need Your help! Please Help me."

He could feel 'lighter' as he'd heard others say. So he started to get up because he was done praying and he could now go and talk to Delta. But just then, he remembered...Delta.

"...Oh yeah...", he quickly knelt back down, and one knee this time, *"...and Lord could You please help Delta pay attention to me and listen to me with a good heart? I don't want to lose her Lord and also, while I am down here, if it work, this is the woman I want to marry."*

James stood up and he was now ready to face Delta.

Delta almost tripped on her slipper and if it wasn't for that leg, she probably would have ran. She didn't want James to know she had heard him praying. Not that she wanted to butt in on any conversation a person was having with the Almighty, but she heard him get loud and start to cry so she wanted to see what was going on.

She really didn't care because she was going in the room to finish him off. She was tired of being tired. She was tired of living the way she was living and she was going in there to give him the boot!

What was this thing he asked the Lord about wanting to marry her? What was wrong with this man? Did he actually think God would grant him that wish if he wasn't taking care of business now?

Either way, she didn't know if that is what she wanted, so she braced herself for this speech because for some reason, she felt she needed to just be still and hear him out this time.

Who knows, she thought, it may be the start of something

A. *Life* Gant

new. A brand new James, who didn't lie,cheat or steal, as he put it when he talked to the Lord. Would he now confess to all his wrong doing and come clean about the other night?

      Delta wondered but at the same time, a feeling of peace and conviction fell on her. The feeling of peace she knew was to help her remain calm in a stormy situation. However, the feelings of conviction was to remind her that she was not perfect nor was she innocent in any shape form or fashion.

      "Alright Dee..." she said to herself, "...shut up and listen to what this man has to say because this is what you have been waiting for. This will be deal breaker for he and you."

      "Baby, you got a minute?"

      The house was quiet. The teenagers were gone. One had spent the night with friends and the other one was with a family member. Her grandchildren left with their mother last night. So this was the best time, if ever.

Chaya's First Death

Chapter Eleven

Momma fussed at daddy the whole way home. It had taken him forever to come and get us, so she was really mad.

Chaya, on the other hand, was so happy to see her daddy that a smile never left her face. When he was around, Chaya was a different girl. She was cheery and loved to talk, at least to him. When he left she was the complete opposite.

Now little Miss Daya was cool all the way around. Rain, sleet or snow, around momma, daddy or the president, she was her usual self, a mess!

"Jacob what took you so long to come and get us? You know mama was going off about any and everything. From the kids and my lifestyle to the house and washing clothes the right way! Where were you?"

Jacob couldn't believe she was questioning him like this because after all, they were not really together anyway. He was just there for the kids and occasionally they would go out on a date, but other than that, she had no right.

"Now Dinah, you don't need to start going off because you don't run me and also because the kids are in the back seat of this car!"

Daddy was a small man in stature but he demanded the respect of a man twice his size and height. He was a milkman. That is how momma met him. He was delivering some milk to my granny and she was home at the time to sign for it. Daddy was also too old for momma, but that didn't stop her, she was "fast" as

A. *Life* Gant

the ole' folks used to say. He was a very hard worker and had been at his same job for nearly eighteen years. He was also in the army reserve. Jacob had other children but since he was paying child support, it didn't matter anyway because at least he did take care of them and she already had one herself. He had just gotten out of a long relationship prior to meeting momma, so their run-in wasn't exactly planned.

Momma was a stone-cold fox and her beauty took Daddy by surprise. He instantly fell for her and she liked what she saw as well.

Time would only tell if they would make it as a couple permanently, but as what was currently taking place at the moment, they argued, fussed and fought too much.

"Dinah you are sitting there yelling and I am the one coming to pick you up! How are you going to act a fool with somebody that's trying to help your ignorant butt? And how did you get over there, to your mama's house anyway? I bet some punk took you over there. Why didn't he stay long enough for you to get the kids ready to go home? He knew he could've waited, now I am up and out all late at night. Shoot! I gotta go to work in the morning!"

Daddy did always jump to conclusions. Probably because deep down inside, he loved Dinah very much but knew it would never work. Jealousy also, almost always, played a huge part in their arguments too.

"Jake", as she'd called him for short, "don't start tripping with me about stuff you know nothing about! You know if my car was working, I wouldn't have to call you. You oughta' be glad that somebody want to put up with your crazy self. And since you wanna know, a cab dropped me off at Mama's house and it would have taken us home too, but I was the last pick-up and mama was going off, which took too long, therefore, the cab left"!

Dinah had her head moving and neck popping as if those actions would make her statements come across to the listener

Chaya's First Death

better.

"I mean do you have a problem coming to get me and Your Kids?"

We were home now and daddy remained silent until Daya and I, were upstairs safely in the apartment. He helped momma get the last of our bags and under his breath, gritting between his teeth, he spoke.

"Dinah, if I had a problem coming to pick you all up, I would not have come in the first place. Don't keep saying that crap in front of my kids. Making them think that I don't love them and wouldn't do nothin' for them! Keep on Dinah, keep on, and..."

He just shut up because he knew him finishing what he had to say would only cause a fight!

"And what...? Huh? And what...? Finish what you were going to say! 'Cause I know you weren't going to say anything about doing something to me?"

Daddy bit his bottom lip which signified that he was on the verge of hitting momma.

"What? You wanna hit me? Hit me! I wish you would!"

Jacob ignored her.

Dinah had a bad mouth, as her mother would always say. She also used to love to egg folk on. Fighting was nothing to her because she would do it in a heartbeat and at the drop of a dime.

Daddy continued to pack our stuff upstairs making sure not to say anything else to 'crazy ol' Dinah. They'd already had too many fights as it was. He dropped us off, gave Daya and I a kiss and left. He had to be at work the next morning.

~~~~~~~~~~~~~~~~

"Five-five-five-zero-zero-seven-seven"

The volume on our phone handset was just as loud as granny's.

Ring, ring, ring, ring, ring.

The phone rang for what seemed like forever to Dinah. "Sadie pick up!" She had so much she wanted to tell Sadie. First she had to finish up telling her about the night at the club and then about her children's father getting on her nerves. Where was she? "Dang, I guess I'll talk to her later then." Dinah sounded so distraught. Who was she going to talk to now? She had other girlfriends but none of them were as close to her as Sadie and there was no one else in the world who she would share so much of her life with. "Oh, well, but I wonder where Say' is? She ain't got no where to go and if she does, I am going to get her for not telling me about it! We tell each other everything! I will just check back with her later."

Dinah would soon find out that what she had been fussing and warning Sadie about, happened!

~~~~~~~~~~~~~~~

"Chaya and Daya, make sure you all brush your teeth and say your prayers before you go to bed".

"O-kaaay", they both replied in sync.

Dinah was raised to make sure she stayed clean and in turn that is what she purposed to do with her children. Delta was a strict when it came to cleaning so Dinah decided she would keep everything just as clean but with half the strictness. She wouldn't know how she did until her children were grown. So she continued doing the best she knew to do with the best of what she had.

~~~~~~~~~~~~~~~

"Man, I wonder what's keeping Sadie?"

Like Delta and her grandmother, Dinah was really blessed with a gift. She could just sense that something good or bad would happen, and usually it did! She just figured God gave her this gift just to have one, really one everybody probably had.

"I sure do want to talk to somebody..."

Just as she was speaking to herself aloud, she could almost swear that she'd heard someone say,

"TALK TO ME", loud and clear.

"Man I need to stop tripping because I'm starting to hear

Chaya's First Death

things and that ain't right!"

She heard it again. This time a little louder but more personal and direct.

" YOU CAN TALK TO ME".

"Okay I don't know what is going on. I keep hearing voices and I know I ain't talkin' to myself like that, am I?"

Now Dinah was beginning to question her sanity. Would her own mind tell her to talk to herself? She thought for a minute. Maybe, because she did talk to herself from time to time and as her grandmother would put it, it was perfectly natural if you didn't respond to yourself! Would she be responding to herself if she gave in to this 'Voice'?

Something must have happened at the club or something else because this ain't right. 'Hearing things' is a reaction to some kinda drug and she certainly didn't do drugs like that! What could this be?

"Well self, if you trying to speak, go on ahead because if you start saying some off the wall stuff, I am cutting you off too!"

Dinah couldn't believe what she was doing.

"Oh my Lord, I am doing what I'd never thought I'd do. I am talking to myself, let me go to bed because I must be tired!"

Dinah brushed her teeth, changed into her pajamas, and went to bed. She rushed off to sleep forgetting to say her prayers, something that was branded in her brain. How could she forget such an important step in her night time rituals?

As a little girl, she remembered talking to God, but this was different. The voice she remembered was still and small, not loud and obnoxious.

Her grandmother, Faizah Love, was a praying woman and she made sure that when she prayed, she did so for her children, her children's children, and so on. Grandma Love as they called her, was a strong woman. She was stricter than Delta, and she did not play games. She rarely played with her kids at all, in any

A. *Life* Gant

capacity, which was the reason Delta let up on her kids and Dinah, hers even more so. She may not have taught them many games to play and she didn't even encourage sports, but she did teach them something that would last them a lifetime and longer. She was very proud of her strength and her ability to take every situation and circumstance to the Lord and that was exactly what she gave out. Instead of games she taught her family to take everything...to the Lord God, Almighty,...in prayer.

Dinah's sleep did not go uninterrupted. She tossed and turned all night. She would wake up every hour on the hour.

Looking at the clock, she could not believe what it read. *2:00am.*

She went back to sleep. Her eyes popped open again. *3:04am.*

She closed her eyes and drifted off into wonderland.

Dinah never had a problem getting to sleep. She could sleep anywhere and at any time. She also never had a problem staying asleep,...until tonight.

Blink. 4:13am!

"What is going on? And why can't I get some freakin' sleep? I have to be at work in the morning to check patients in and without sleep I won't even be able to read the charts".

She was frustrated now. Her job at the doctor's office was pretty decent and she had a good rapport with the patients too.

"*Zzzzzz whooo, Zzzzzz whooo!*"

That whistling in her sleep was annoying, and thank God no one had to hear it!

Blink, Blink. The digital clock display read *4:18am.*

"Four- eighteen!!! Okay Lord. Now I remember when Mama used to say You woke her up early in the morning when You had somethin' to say. So shoot! But first, please assure me it is You I am talkin' to. I am crazy enough as it is."

"Talk to Me and I will Talk to you!"

Tears began to flow down the sides of her face. She laid

~*87*~

Chaya's First Death

there thinking and wondering how she could mistake the voice of the Lord for something so trivial as her mind or even worse, drugs!

"Yes, Lord. I am awake and I hear You loud and clear. What are You trying to say to me and what do You need me to do?"

Dinah heard again...

"You can talk to Me and I will talk to you."

This time the voice was much softer, like she remembered as a little girl. It was then that she knew God simply just wanted her to pray. Pray for the first time in a long time!

"Well Lord, first of all, I would like to thank You for everything You have done for me. If it had not been for You I don't know where I would be. What I do know is that You have been there for me all the time. Even when I didn't deserve Your mercy and Your grace, You kept me Lord! And I thank You! I thank You for waking me up this morning. I thank You for letting me see another day. I thank You for healthy children. I thank You Lord for forgiving me..."

Dinah wept sore. She had a lot to be forgiven of, she thought.

"...forgiving a wretch like me. Lord You watch over me day and night and I thank You! I don't know what else to say Lord, but please forgive me and help me do what You want me to do! Thank You in advance. In Jesus' name I pray, Amen."

She fell asleep and finally got some rest, even though it was only for two hours!

A. *Life* Gant

Chapter Twelve

At work all Dinah could think about was her friend Sadie. Her insides felt as if they had been beaten with a meat cleaver of worry. Why hadn't Sadie called her? She knew that there was nothing they hid from one another. Maybe Say' needed some space. This time of silence had happened somewhat, before. But at least her best friend called her and let her know that she would call her when she was ready to talk. Could it be her stupid boyfriend? The last time it was. Hopefully it is not something too bad, Dinah thought.

"It better not be nothing crazy. 'Cause I'll tear up hell and whatever else standing in the way about my partner!"

Dinah only realized her thoughts became vocal when her co-worker looked at her with eyes as big as silver dollars. Still she didn't care. She continued to do her job while worrying. Her work didn't suffer and nobody even knew it.

Dinah was one of those people who never allowed the world to know she was shaken up about anything. She taught her children the same technique. Daya picked it up. But with Chaya, it was a little harder to teach and she would carry her worries with her into her adult life.

Dinah would often tell her girls...

"Babies, never let the enemy see you sweat, 'Cause if he see that what he's doing is causing you to waver or be scared, he is going to try his best to knock you on over and out! Y'all hear me?"

~*89*~

Chaya's First Death

"Yes ma'am."

Dinah could still hear the voices of her babies and it made her smile. Yet she still couldn't shake her bad feeling that something was up with her best friend, Sadie. Of course she knew what to do, as God had reminded her to do it last night...

"...Talk to Him...!

And that is what she did.

~~~~~~~~~~~~

"Please Officer, can you tell me where they are? I need to know where my children are! Pleeease, Pleeease, let me speak to my children!"

"Ma'am you are going to have to calm down. Your children are safe and that is all the information I can give you at this time. You will have to come down to the station for questioning.

Sadie was a wreck. Something had happened to her children and no one, not even the police department would let her know anything until she went down to the station. But how would she get there? Her car was out of gas and she didn't have any money.

She could call her parents, but they could be in on this. They would be the main ones telling her how unfit of a mother they thought she was and how she just needed to give the kids over to somebody 'more fit' than she was.

Or...she could call her best friend Dinah, or not... What would Dinah say to her? Would she say "I told you so"? No she couldn't call her either.

Who could she call, she had nobody except...her low-down boyfriend, William.

Frantically, Sadie dialed William's phone number. She could barely hold onto the phone because she was shaking violently.

"Hello?"

William's deep baritone voice always made her stomach

A. *Life* Gant

quiver but not today. It actually made her extremely fearful because it reminded her of the officer's voice she spoke to earlier. She didn't know what to say to him about the problem at hand and she was afraid of what he might think of her.

"H-Hello? Will it's me, Sad..."

Sadie couldn't even finish introducing herself because the sobs replaced her words. She tried to speak but couldn't and it made Will worry.

"Say' what's wrong with you? Why are you crying?"

The only thing coming from Sadie's end of the phone was screaming and wailing as if she was being murdered at that very moment.

"Say' I can not understand you with you crying and all that! Please calm down so you can tell me what's going on!"

William began to grow tired of her crying so he pleaded with her the more.

"Will, they took my babies and I don't know where they at! The police want me to come down to the station for questioning and I don't have a way. My parents won't help me and I just need you to come and get me to take me downtown. Will I would not have asked you if I didn't need you. I could take myself but I don't have any gas money or bus fare. Do you think you can come and get me or drop some money off for gas? I will pay you back."

"Ssh, Ssh"

Will was shoosing another woman who happened to be at his house and stupid Sadie didn't even realize that he wasn't talking to her.

"Huh? I'm quiet now. Did you hear me?"

"Yes, Say' I hear you but let me get something straight. You said somebody's got your kids and you don't know where they are? Your mama ain't got them or nobody in your family? And they are where? At the police station right and you want me to take you and pick them up?

William knew he was not listening. He was too busy with

~91~

Chaya's First Death

the distraction of another woman.

"NO Will! I said I need you take Meee... to the station so I could see what's going on with my kids. Something has happened and I need to find out. So...can you take me? Or not?"

"Well actually Sadie I'm sorry. I can't help you right now because I am tied up at this very moment."

"What did you say Will? You can't be serious, can you? My children are sitting somewhere wondering when and if I am coming to get them and all you can come up with is you are tied up? What Will'? What? Are you tied up over there with some other woman? Huh?"

Sadie began to cry again because now it dawned on her that the shooshing he was doing earlier was not for her. It was directed towards a lady at his apartment.

Will had hung up the other end just as she was about to start begging.

"Hello? Hello? Will? Will?"

Sadie slammed the phone down and and picked it up again to redial his number, but there was no answer, the phone had kept ringing as if he'd turned the ringer off.

"What am I going to do now? I don't have anybody else. Let me see if I can find some change around here somewhere. If I can scrape up enough, maybe I can walk to the store with the gas can, fill it up and then get somebody to drop me back by the house."

Sadie had it all figured out and she did exactly as she had planned. Only it took longer than rehearsed.

The route to the corner store was not an easy one. She had to walk through some sticka' bushes and up a steep, gravel hill. She also had to watch out for stray dogs, ones that would definitely chase you if you got close. Which is exactly what happened to Sadie.

"Excuse me sir, do you think you could give me a ride around the corner? I don't want to walk that far with the little bit of gas I've got. Plus, I can't run from those dogs with it either."

"No ma'am, I don't think so. I don't want that gas smell in my car."

Sadie went on asking every person she felt looked nice enough. The only problem was that no one wanted to give her a ride with gasoline in hand.

She did what she had to do...and walked home. This time she would do all she could to deter the rabid dogs and go another route. The long way.

~~~~~~~~~~~~~

"I am Mrs. Thomas from the Department of Human Services and I have come to retrieve the children believed to be in an abusive situation."

She showed her badge of authenticity.

"Yes Ma'am, My name is Officer Petty and the children you are referring to have been found by themselves in an unfit environment. Their mother has left them alone on numerous occasions and neither of them is old enough to take care of the other's needs."

The officer leaned in closer as if to tell her a secret.

"Now you know the oldest one, who is only eleven years old was caught in bed with a twenty-one year old man. We are still investigating whether or not it was consensual. The man said that the young lady lied about her age. Although she does look older than many, many girls her age, the courts will most likely convict him of rape."

The DHS representative shook her head in disbelief. She had a niece that age and couldn't imagine anything like that happening to her. As Mrs. Thomas began her own form of interrogation, a small framed, black lady came up to the front desk and asked where her grandchildren were. That lady was Sadie's mother, Mrs. Edwards.

"Excuse me. Excuse me, Miss!"

The clerk answered her after she hung up the phone.

Chaya's First Death

"My name is Tonya Edwards and I believe you have my grandchildren here or somewhere. And whoever it was that called me said something about my oldest granddaughter being raped or something like that. Can you tell me what's going on.....?"

Officer Petty interrupted her frantic behavior and began to question her.

"Now you say you are their grandmother? Would you describe the victim please. Anyone can come in and claim some children or property, but without a description, I can not or will not allow you to do so much as peek through a window at them."

"Well my oldest grand baby is about yea tall..."

Sadie's mom raised an arm up as if to describe her height, but she really had no idea. She claimed to be this spectacular grandmother but she knew that was a lie. The only times she saw the kids was on their birthdays and holidays. The few times in between was when she called herself teaching Sadie a lesson, one Mrs. Edwards prayed she'd learn fast, because she was too old to raise anymore children.

"Okay, Miss.....?"

"It's Mizzus Edwards."

She interjected.

"Okay then, Mizzus Edwards, and thank you for clearing that up. Now where were you at the time of the incident?"

The officer had already made her mad by not knowing her name and now he was getting in her business. Why did he need to know? She thought to herself.

Just as she was about to speak and as if he heard her, he held up his pen to stop her.

"We need to know this type of information so we can rule out any unneeded and unuseful information. Is that clear enough?"

She nodded and began to blurt out whatever she thought would be helpful, keeping in mind not to appear that she really didn't care for the most part about the well-being of her only grandchildren. She did care but she made it clear on several occasions that she was extremely unhappy about her daughter having children in the first place.

"Iiiii seee."

Mrs. Edwards didn't like the long drawn out version of his last response. It sounded like he didn't believe her and she was getting more ticked off by the second.

"If so, why weren't you looking after them while their mother was away? It shows here that you actually live only a couple of blocks away?

She nodded, which meant he was correct.

He continued. "Can you give me a reason Mrs. Edwards? Why weren't they at your home?

When she didn't answer his question he changed the subject.

"Mrs. Edwards, what is the relationship like between you and the victim's mother?

"It's FINE!" She quickly yelled not realizing she had done so.

"Okay, I sense you and your daughter's relationship is a touchy subject because of your uneasiness about this whole situation. Anyway, thank you for your cooperation. If we need to ask you any further questions, we know how to contact you. Again, thank you and have a good one."

Officer Petty tipped his hat to her and began to walk off.

"Wait! Aren't you going to let me see my grandchildren?"

"I'm afraid not ma'am. It has been made known to me that they do not want to see you."

Sadie's mother stood in the hallway in disbelief and down her cheek came one lonely tear.

~~~~~~~~~~~~~

Sadie made it home, but not unharmed though. Those dogs tore into her and she would definitely need a tetanus shot. However, the bites were the least of her worries.

Chaya's First Death

"God I wish I had somebody to call. It's getting dark and I really do need to see my kids."

She didn't mean for this to happen. Of course no one does, she thought. Had she really been too careless with them in leaving her children at home alone as Dinah had said? But she still saw nothing wrong with it because she was done the same way as a child and she thought she turned out okay. Besides her girls were eleven, five and three. Her oldest was mature enough to babysit for just a few hours at a time. The problem was the few hours turned into several and on occasion, overnight! Her mind started racing with all the possibilities of what might have happened and tears flowed down her round, ebony-colored face.

"Oh no! I need to call the police station and tell them I am still coming. I just had to get some gas and ..."

"Police Department, how may I help you?"

"Uh...yes this is uh...Sadie Thomas and I would like to speak to uh..."

She pulled out the old receipt she wrote his name on.

"Uh...Officer Petty? Yeah that's it. I need to tell him I am still coming. I was having car trouble but I am on my..."

"Uh...Yes Miss Thomas I know who you are but unfortunately Officer Petty has turned the custody of your children over to state's Department of Human Services. And it shows here that your court date is scheduled for..."

"Noooo...NOT MY BABIES!!!!! NOOOO!!!!!! Please Ma'am I'll do anything. Just please don't take my babies. They are all I've got! But can you at least let me know what happened? I just need to know!"

The clerk wasn't able to finish because Sadie let out the most painful cry she had ever heard. A cry which said this was an accident and she was sorry for what happened. Something she still had no idea of.

"I am not at liberty to share those details with you over the phone but you can call this number and speak to the worker in

A. *Life* Gant

charge of your case."
"I'm sorry Ma'am but share? I am not asking you to give me something as meaningless as a piece of candy. I want to know about my babies...forget it! Could you repeat that number again for me?"

Chaya's First Death

Chapter Thirteen

    Chaya had forgotten all about what happened to her play cousins when they were young. The only thing she could think to do now was raise her hands in praise as if to say "Thank you Lord. What happened to Aunt Sadie's kids may have happened to us if it weren't for Mama. Momma was wild no doubt but we did at least have someone taking care of us whether they wanted to or not."

    It was now one o'clock in the morning and Chaya new she had to get some rest. She wouldn't be any good to anyone without it. So she did a once over of her house again. She went upstairs to check on her babies and peeked in their room, quietly. She smiled as she looked at her girls knocked out and sprawled across the bed. The funniest part was that they reminded her soo much of her and Daya as children.

    Coy, like her mother had always wanted her own space. And she tried to keep it that way to deter Beta, who was a lot like her aunt Daya. But Beta somehow always managed to weasel her way into bed with her older sister, complaining that she was too scared to sleep alone. Coy and Chaya hated sharing their sleeping space with their younger sisters Beta and Daya, because they slept like they were akin to the octopus, arms and legs everywhere!

    She smiled again and slowly shut the door. Her tears ran their usual course. They should have payed the mortgage or at least rent on her face, they were there so often. This time the tears were not sad ones, at least not at first.

A. *Life* Gant

    Chaya made her way back downstairs towards the kitchen to clean up her mess but decided against it. Instead she went back to her room, disrobed and wondered what else God was going to say in dream form. She had really hoped He would change His way of getting her attention to daytime hours, but if she would slow her butt down He could speak then as well.

    Climbing into bed beside her husband, his musky scent brought back memories of the earlier, happier times.

~~~~~~~~~~~~~

    "Breath into me Oh Lord,...the breath of life,...so that my spirit can be whole... and my soul made right..."

    The melodious sounds of Fred Hammond was among her favorite and his too.

    "Where did you get that song I like it? Can I borrow that tape so I can listen to it at home? I'll give it back."

    Joshua Jackson fell in love with Chaya Smith the minute he laid eyes on her. He knew she was to be his wife. He would give her anything she asked him for. Whether it was the shirt off his back, the jacket he wore to work because she was cold, or in this case, his favorite cassette tape.

    "Yeah you can keep it, I have another one somewhere at the house."

    She would know eventually that he was lying just to please her.

    Chaya grinned from ear to ear as she thought how she would clean her apartment listening to the new-used addition to her music collection.

    "Thanks Josh'. Can I call you Josh'?"

    He leaned back in the driver's seat of his silver, Oldsmobile Cutlass Supreme and smiled at the thought of his new soon-to-be, girlfriend's request for a name change.

    "Yeah that's cool. You can call me 'J' too, if you want. My brothers call me that for short."

    Chaya was love stricken herself. This man appeared to

Chaya's First Death

have close to the total package. He was cute, he had a beautiful smile, and he would give her anything. Aside from the fact that he was slightly on the burly side, he adored her and it didn't matter if he had three kids already. She herself had one as well, so she didn't trip and it would remain that way if his baby's mother stayed in her place.

"Okay and thanks for lunch, it was pretty good. Although...." she smiled, "I ain't going back there because the grease alone will kill you!"

Both lovebirds cracked up at the last comment because it was true. The Freeze Stop, a place she'd heard about as a child, was ran by an older couple who apparently thought the greasier the food the better.

"You are very welcome, Chay'. It was my pleasure. Maybe we can go again sometime."

He laughed at the widening of her tight, Asian-like eyes.

"I mean maybe somewhere else?"

Chaya happily agreed and blushed at the fact that he'd already given her a pet name. Even though that is what everyone who knew her well, called her anyway.

~~~~~~~~~~~~~

"Excuse me, but my buddy would like to know your situation."

If looks were used as deadly weapons, Joshua would have been dead and Chaya would have gone to prison for homicide.

"What?"

"Dang Girl, I am just trying to ask you your name so I can hook up my boy."

Joshua started off lying which later would be cute to her.

"Who is yo' boy and why didn't he step to me like a man himself? I don't do kids' games, I already have one of them at home."

Chaya was a mess but she was not up for any games. Her daughter's donor, as she liked to put it, was sorry and she didn't

A. *Life* Gant

want to go there with another joker.

Joshua had a pretty smile she thought and really hoped he was the 'boy' he lied about. What she didn't know yet was that he was. And his smile was a reaction to his learning of her having a baby. That meant she wouldn't judge him too much for having three.

"I will let him know and can I get your name so I can have, I mean so I can go and tell him that too?"

"Chaya. Chaya Smith. Is that it because I'm new here and I don't think the boss would be happy with us chatting away like this?"

"Yes, but do me a favor and smile more. It looks good on you!"

What Josh didn't know was that Chaya was a broken vessel and she leaked. The issues from her painful past flowed from the frowns on her face. But at the request of her co-worker and unknowingly soon-to-be boyfriend, she smiled but only after a quick, ornery frown.

~~~~~~~~~~~~~~~~

Chaya resorted to the fact that she wasn't going to get any sleep. She still smiled, and thought to herself, where had the man she fell in love with gone? Yes, he was still sweet and kind. He still adored her but where had the father figure in him gone? She knew that most girls marry men like their father and she did just that, she thought. What happened to him taking care of every one of her heart's desires, big or small? Her daddy did that and her husband was to take over in that department once she got married, or was that a figment of her imagination? Had she been duped?

"What happened to us J'?"

She silently asked her sleeping husband. Of course he wasn't going to respond but a little part of her wanted him to.

"I mean we were so happy and now look at us? We both lead two separate lives. Our roles as husband and wife have been drastically reversed in a non-traditional sort of way. I love

Chaya's First Death

working and doing what I do but not at the expense of my mind running away from me. It's not even a matter of who makes more money because you know that's not an issue either. It's what you do with what you make. I just pray we can make this work because the way everything looks, it's kind of hard to see the good in it. I know you are asleep but I am talking to your spirit right now and I pray that you rise up and do what you are called to do as a man. A man of God who is a great husband, a wonderful father, and one who has an entrepreneurial spirit."

    Chaya spoke all this to her gentle, sleeping giant because she thought he was doing just that...sleeping! Little did she know, he had quietly gotten up to go and relieve himself while she was making tea. Joshua was awake the whole time!

Chapter Fourteen

James knelt down in front of the chair she was sitting in, grabbed her hand and with tears in his eyes, he spoke.

"First of all, Delta baby, I want to say I am sorry for everything I've done. I have not been completely honest with you. I know better than to treat you any kind of way. You are a beautiful, strong woman and I don't deserve to be with a lady of your caliber."

Reminding herself of the vow she'd made earlier she sat still so she could hear what he had to say, wondering when the real truth was going to come out.

"I have constantly taken your kindness for weakness and I'm sorry. You have done for me what no woman has ever done this long, you have stuck by me when no one else would..."

Delta could feel herself wanting to butt in and tell him he wasn't lying, but she decided against it and let him finish.

By the look on Delta's face and her body language, James could tell her patience was wearing thin so he spoke with more of a sense of urgency.

"...You are the kinda' woman that a man can fall in love with easy and that is what I've done. Delta I love you and can not imagine my world without you.But I know I have to get some things straightened out before I can expect you to ever love me the way that I love you."

Beads of sweat had begun to form on James' forehead and nose which was an indication that he was extremely nervous. Sure

Chaya's First Death

he had reason because Delta's strength was intimidating for male or female.

"...I'ma get straight to the point..."

"Fi-na-lly!"

Delta kept this thought to herself.

"...On last Saturday...when you sent me to the store to pick up the beer,...I did just that! Only problem was that we had to wait on the little guy to come out of the back with the beer. See what had happened was, when we got to the store and looked in the ice box, all the beer you liked was gone so he went to the back of the store to check and see if they had some more. They did but anyway...while we were waiting on him and while me and Tommy were talking, Tony and some of his men came in and held us up."

"What did you say? Oh my God! You were held up and you didn't tell me? Who in the hell is Tony?"

Delta was undone and anticipated the rest of the story because now she couldn't sit still in her seat.

"Baby hold on, let me finish. As I was saying, He held us up with guns and..."

"Guns? James hurry up 'cause you makin' my presha' rise!"

"Del' let me finish! Tony is the guy I owe some money to and he saw the truck..."

"That ugly a** truck...yeah, yeah I'll let you finish"

Delta was through and prayed that what this man had left to say would not send her to an early grave.

By now James was getting fed up with her interrupting him and he made the decision to speak faster. This time non-stop!

"Del' I owe Tony eighteen hundred dollars because he thought I was lying about my payday and he made it double. It was nine hundred and I had no idea he was going to double it! He said I got until this Friday to pay him or he coming to get me or maybe something or somebody that is dear to me. But don't worry I get paid this Friday and I am going to see if my brother will loan

A. *Life* Gant

me the rest."

"I can't believe you are going to expect me to sit hear and not say anything about this! What the hell is wrong with you James? I thought that you were in some mess, but this...? And do you honestly think that your brother will be able to just let you borrow some money? How many hours of overtime did you work this week? 'Cause you think you was working then...just waaaait...YOU GONE BE ONE TIRED S.O.B!!!!! I ain't got no money and don't expect me to come up off none either! James what's your plan? Please tell me you got a plan. If that man even think about coming up over here to take something of mine, you ain't got to worry about him killing you because I' m going to do it my da** self!"

James knew he was in trouble because not only did he have a loan shark ready to kill him but Delta his woman, did have a gun and she wasn't afraid to use it either. She shot at him three months ago when he lost his mind for a short while thinking he was going to put his hands on her.

"Now how long you say you got to pay this man off? 'Cause if you talking about in two days this Friday you got some work to do! Ooh...Lord help me today 'cause I can't do it no more."

Delta was on a roll now. One minute she prayed and the next minute she was going off. Besides what was he supposed to say about his past actions that now have become present problems? He just kept silent and let her get whatever she needed to say off her chest. What her long-time boyfriend was really hoping was that she would calm down between now and then and if his brother didn't have the money to help him, maybe just maybe he could get it from her.

The situation at hand was too much for her to handle. She went into the bedroom to get her daily pill organizer. Her blood pressure was up and she knew for certain she needed to calm down. Delta sat down on the edge of the bed and with the half-full

Chaya's First Death

glass of luke-warm water, she took her medication. Going to the hospital was an event she did not want to be the planner of so she took an extra pill for good measure.

When the effect of the meds began to take place, Delta felt the need to do something she had not done in years, only this time it wasn't just praying. It was getting down on bended knees to pray! When this thought arose, she had to make sure it was the Lord encouraging her to do so, because the accident left her lower body pretty weak. She slowly and strategically turned on her side while on her bed and then slid down to the floor.

"Now Lord, You know I need Your help. I don't know what to do. Please help me do the right thing. If You can show me the way..."

She continued praying for over an hour.

James was always scared when Delta got to talking to the Lord. Especially when what she talked to Him about was him and his mess. So he figured he would counteract or pray against whatever Delta prayed about that had to do with him.

"Lord please don't do whatever she is trying to get You to do in any area that concerns me. In Jesus' name Amen."

James obviously didn't understand how the Almighty worked. But he would soon find out that He definitely didn't work against Himself!

~~~~~~~~~~~~~~~

"Man let's roll by and see what that punk James is up to. 'See if he's doing what he needs to do to get my money."

Tony and his buddies were bored and they decided to make an early trip to see their friend James as a scare tactic.

Driving up to Delta's house made the three guys uneasy because they'd heard that although small in stature, she was a crazy woman. Nevertheless, they pressed on. Upon their arrival, they saw James outside on the porch smoking a cigarette. James wanted to run and hide but he didn't want to appear as a coward in front of his woman. They called to him from the car in the street.

A. *Life* Gant

"Hey man what's up? You take care of what we talked about because I mean what I said?"

Tony obviously didn't know whose home he was at because Delta never appreciated unwelcomed visitors.

Looking around at his surroundings and to make sure Delta was not in the vicinity, James spoke in a very low almost under breath tone.

"I told you I didn't get paid 'til this Friday. But I am going to need more time. I will have what I owe you but since you doubled it I'm still working on that. Man I need you to cut me a break. Don't you think you are being unreasonable? I mean besides, is it my fault that you got the dates mixed up?"

James was being gutsy, maybe because Delta was home, but nevertheless, gutsy. He knew that this man, although a real coward, could mop the floor with him. This loan shark was getting pretty upset by the words of the person who owed him money and tried to refrain from roughing him up but now it was becoming difficult.

"So seriously Tony, are you going to cut me some slack? I can guarantee this will be the last time I need to come to you for some cash because I promised my woman that I would get myself together so can you help a brotha' out?"

Tony laughed until tears came down his stubble-haired cheeks.

"You must not know who you are talking to. I can take you out with one word and keep my hands clean. But on the issue of my money, I could be generous and reduce the interest but since you stuck your foot in your mouth with all this jive talk, I ain't! I will be back Friday or you can come to me. You know where to find me!"

After speaking, he peeled off and the smell of burnt rubber caused James' head to hurt. Or was it the fear that had already began to overtake him?

Chaya's First Death

"Precious, Lord...Take my hand...Lead me on...and Let me stand...I am tired and I am weak...I am worn...Through the storms...Through the night...Lead me on...To the light...Take my hand...Precious Lord and Lead me ON!..."

Delta sang while she vacuumed her living room. This was one of her favorite gospel songs and it had come to mind at the perfect time, the time when she needed Him to take her hand and lead her.

James walked into the house and his accidental slamming of the screen door, startled her. If it had not been for the praises she just sent up and the great feelings they gave her, Delta would have cursed him out.

"James, I saw you out there talking to those guys. Was one of them that Tony guy?"

"Yeah baby", he sadly said.

"What's wrong with you? Did they do something or say something to you?"

"Naw baby, they were just stopping by to mess with me. 'Trying to see if I was going to have that money I owe. But I'm cool. I need to go and call my brother right quick to see if he can help me out..."

"Alright do whatcha gotta' do!"

Delta didn't want to sound cruel but she was past tired of playing games with men.

A. *Life* Gant

Chapter Fifteen

"Who is it?" Dinah yelled. She wasn't expecting any company.
"Knock, knock, knock!"
"Who is it? Unless you identify yourself you ain't getting in."

Dinah looked at the clock on her wall, it read 11:33 p.m. and wondered who was coming over to her house at this time of night.

"It's me!"
"Me who?"
She played crazy. She knew who it was.
"It's me, Mister! Girl quit playing, you know it is."

Dinah slowly opened the door and let him in. She gave him a look as if to question his presence at her home.

Without hesitation, he began to grope her and she didn't stop him. This was what she longed for. A man's touch. Even if it did come from Mister. While he caressed her body, she inhaled his scent and her mind took her back to that night at the club. Yanking from his grasp, she screamed and pushed him away.

"What's wrong with you girl? Why are you tripping? I haven't seen you in days and you acting like you don't want to see me!"

Mister's voice softened and he stepped closer to her.
"What baby, you didn't miss me? Huh? 'Cause I missed you."

Chaya's First Death

Dinah tried her best not to succumb to his sweet talk. It was getting harder by the second. She loved the attention men gave her but she knew better than to allow him to come back after what he did at the club. How could he stand there and think that his actions were okay?

"Yeah, I missed you but I would be less than the woman I was raised to be if I keep letting you walk all over me and be with other women! Would you take me back if you saw me leave the club with another man? Huh? I don't think so!"

"But I did see you dancing with one. What do you have to say about that? Am I supposed to be happy about that?"

"Boy you better shut-up because dancing with a man and leaving with a woman are two different things! Did I or did I not see you leave with another woman? And on top of that, you had the nerve to be rude and walk off while I was speaking. That's messed up Mister, how could you? And to think I loved you? You know what I ain't even mad at you, I'm mad at myself. I have allowed you to come up in here like you have done nothing wrong. You left with her and do you think that's okay with me?"

"Baby, I didn't do nothing with her. We just went to get something to eat and then we went to her house to watch some t.v. that is it!"

"Please shut up! I don't know how much of this I can take. You mean to tell me that not only did you leave with her, but you took her to get something to eat? Punk you don't even take me nowhere! Every time I suggest going somewhere like the club, out to eat or to the movies, you act like you are too tired to go or you have to work! Puh-leaze! Get out my face!"

"Dee, Baby, please, please don't act like that! I love you! What do you think I came over here for? I came to apologize for what I've been doing and the way I've been acting. Please forgive me."

Mister was now on his knees and Dinah's heart became as putty in his hands. She didn't want to love him back but she did.

A tear formed in her right eye and he knew he had her then.

"I know why you came over here Mister, you came because that tramp you left the club with, put you out and now you ain't got nowhere to go! Am I just a piece of tail to you? You don't treat people you love that way. When you love someone, you see them all the time, you don't stay gone for days at a time and then show up! Not to the one you love! Mister when you love somebody, no let me change that, when and if you loved me, you wouldn't treat me as you do."

"How do I treat you? I treat you good. How are you going to say that I treat you any other way?"

Mister thought by now he would've been in. But Dinah was playing hard to get which was getting on his nerves!

"Now you patronizing me. You keep asking me how I think you are treating me and I keep telling you like crap! But as I said before, I take the blame for it, because I let you do it! But not again. No more will I let you use and abuse me like you have been. I am worth more than the crap you put me through. And what are you apologizing for? Didn't you say you didn't do nothing?"

Mister was busted! What did he do or better yet what did he do that he was willing to confess to?

"Umm...what are you talking about? I didn't apologize for nothing but leaving the club and stuff...and I don't think there was nothing else."

He was stuttering and Dinah went off, sounding just like her mother Delta.

"What did you do? Did you sleep with her? And you better not lie to me!"

The clock read 1:16a.m.

Dinah was tired and she wanted to go to bed but the information about to be revealed was far more important to her at the time.

"Please let me explain. I did not...mean for this to happen.

Chaya's First Death

I wanted to make you jealous so I did what I did."

"You still have yet to make me understand what it was that you did not mean for it to happen? And plus what was I doing that made you jealous enough to try and make me jealous in return?"

"Well...you was dancing with that dude like I wasn't even there...and..."

Dinah broke in loudly.

"Did I go to the club with you?"

"No you didn't, but you knew I was going to be there. And like I was sayin'..."

"What!? How am I supposed to know you are going to be somewhere when you barely even tell me where you are going? We don't do anything, so I figured either you were always lying or busy. I chose to believe you were busy because at least it sounded better when somebody asked where you were."

Still avoiding the obvious, the fact that he had to come clean about his whereabouts, scared the mess out of Mister. Now he was mentally rehearsing the new lie he thought he was going to tell. Little did he know that Dinah was no fool. She had been in his position as a cheater before so there really wasn't a lie he'd tell that she hadn't already used.

"Okay Miss know-it-all, you told me long time ago that you didn't want anything long-term and I did. Because of that statement I assumed we could do what we wanted with who we wanted. Without any repercussions. Am I right or am I wrong? So...yes. I did sleep with her and I am sorry if that is a problem for you. But I did. I can promise you that I won't do that again with her. But I can't promise you that I won't be with anybody else because you, yourself don't want a relationship. Now if you can promise me that you won't be with anyone other than me, I will do my best to stay true as well. So what do you say?"

Dinah was flabbergasted. Here this guy was, telling her he slept with another woman because she didn't want a relationship and asking for her to be faithful to his lying butt all in the same breath. She had to have been dreaming and unaware that her thoughts became vocal, she said,...

"Somebody pinch me so I can wake up from this nightmare!"

"What are you talking about baby? What nightmare?"

"It's too late to keep talking to you, besides I have to get some rest for work tomorrow! The nightmare I'm referring to is the one where you come to me, acting like everything is alright even though I haven't seen you for days, tell me that the lady you left me for, you slept with, and then you want me to declare that I'm your woman? Goooood Night! I am going to bed! You can sleep on the couch because I am just nice enough to let you. Seeing that it is almost two a.m. and you don't need to be driving."

"Babe, you can't be serious. Sleep on the couch?"

"Hell yes! I'm serious! You ain't sleeping in my bed!"

Mister tossed and turned on the couch for the next few hours. He was too tall for one and it was actually a love seat with a recliner on the end of it. Kicking the blanket that she gave him off his legs, he became frustrated and sat up. Before he realized what he was doing, he had already slid into bed with Dinah.

Dinah was used to having him in her bed so it was only natural for an arm to land on his chest while she was sleeping. To him this was a sign that she had forgiven him of his lustful sins.

"Good morning sweetheart, I'm sorry."

He kissed her on the forehead and she snuggled up to him. When she didn't respond, he repeated himself.

"Good morning baby, I'm sorry".

"Umhuh", she mumbled in agreement and inhaled the scent of her man.

"If things could be this way all the time", she thought.

Chaya's First Death

"Was this the same man that just hours ago, confessed the crime of the century? I need to get myself together also, since I was pointing the finger. I'm no better than he is and I can't talk so I'll just exhale and chill...with my man."

Dinah had just lost her emotional mind. She was the same woman who told her best girlfriends to drop a man who was no good. And here she was doing exactly what she warned them about, only worse. Her friends' men could just look at them wrong and Dinah wasn't having it. Yet her beau had slept with another broad and she was all wrapped up with him. If only one of them could see her now. Their buddy who was an advocate for women's rights, so to speak.

Dinah Marie needed some of old Delta's chastisement. Not that her mother's mouth was the prayerbook on this issue, it was one of her kind of talks that would shut Dinah down. Just long enough to make her think. Or maybe even Sadie, her best friend, who'd put her on a pedestal, which Dinah hated, but that too would do the job.

A tiny tap on the door interrupted previous thoughts of any action taking place.

"Tap, tap, tap. Tap, tap, tap."

Possum was seriously being played in momma's room. The knocking didn't help so Chaya made the grown-up decision to open the door, unannounced.

To her surprise, momma was half covered up and half not. The memory of the showcase's display would be forever branded in her mind.

"Momma, momma?"

Chaya whispered as not to disturb neither of the two artifacts which seemed as if they were behind a glass case in a museum.

"Oh well, I guess momma didn't hear me."

She walked out of the room not only saddened by what she saw but because her mother promised to make her 'pretty' for

A. *Life* Gant

school pictures today.

Her young mind began to wander down the road of what if's and why's.

"What if momma's boyfriend didn't come over last night? Would me and Beta's hair be done up real pretty? What if she would have stuck to her guns about not wanting a 'cheater'? Would she be happy with just us or mean again because it was just us? Why was momma doing this to herself and us? Hadn't we all suffered enough when we became attached to the last boyfriend? Why did momma think it was okay to act this way in front of her two little women? Was this the same behavior we would mimic as adults or even sooner? How long would this last and would she be that beacon of light to show us the way? Would she be that example for us to know that no matter how many times you fall it is the getting back up that counts?" Hopefully so, but only time would answer her questions.

"Beta come onnn." Chaya sang.

She had to brush her baby sister's hair up into a ponytail before school. Beta was not an early riser like her big sister, so she had to be practically drug out of bed. Chaya went into the kitchen to get a cup of warm water. She saw her momma dip the brush in it so the water on the brush could mix with the grease already placed in the hair. Returning back to the shared bedroom, Chaya viewed her half-sleep, half-awake sister fumbling with the strings on her shoes. The girls argued a little about who did it best, but Chaya ended up tying Beta's shoes, after which, she brushed her hair as well, making it pretty enough, she thought, for picture day.

Chaya's First Death

Chapter Sixteen

Chaya woke up in a cold sweat. Her pillows were wet from sweat and tears. Blood may have followed if she had swung violently like she did in the past. Why did she continue to have these day and nightmares. The last one she had had was about her mother Dinah not being available for one important day in her school-aged life. This meant a lot to her because it was picture day and since it was the last year she'd spend in elementary school, it was to never be forgotten. Her daddy promised to buy her a yearbook and she would keep it for the rest of her life.

Laying beside her praying that what he had just witnessed was not somehow indirectly related to him, Joshua wrapped his arm around her waist and softly pulled himself closer. When she began to resist, slapping his carousing hand, it was then that he knew the dream was either about him or had something to do with him. He didn't waist any time jumping in to save her thoughts of him.

"Baby, you alright? What were you dreaming about? Because when I tried to hold you, you smacked my hand! What was that all about? It was about me huh? The dream was about me." Joshua's voice faded at his last question and answer statements.

"Yea I'm alright. Just had another one of those dreams about my past."

"What do you mean your past and who was in it?"

A. *Life* Gant

    Chaya knew that if she looked at his pitiful face while he asked a silly thing like that, she would have gone into a fit of rage. Here she was, his wife, having terrible nightmares and night tares about her childhood, and all he could worry about was if the dream somehow enclosed a past relationship with another man. How stupid was he? Trying to hold her composure, and not say something that would lead to another argument, Chaya looked at her husband, her eyes said it all but she let her mouth do the talking. "J' is something wrong with you? Are you okay? Obviously not, because only a fool without a heart would ask a question like that already knowing the answer."

    "What are you talking about? You are the one who is always having these dreams about stuff! How am supposed to know what they are about? Shoot one time, no I change that, several times, you have woke me up out of my sleep hitting on me because of some flashback you was havin' about some stupid dude who used to hit you! We ain't gone talk about the time your little brother walked in the room one night to get something, only to find your hand around my neck! So yeah! I have a right and reason to ask you what your dream was about so I'll know when to duck!" Josh was ticked off and since he put it that way, she could surely understand where he was coming from.

    "Well I'm sorry if I have put you through Sooo much heartache and pain..." Chaya was being smart. "...No really, you already know that for the past few months I have been having these reoccurring dreams about my childhood. I don't know why but I think God is trying to show me something or teach me something. I do believe they are in some way meant to bring healing because some of the things I experienced and saw, are now somehow directly related to the present as it stands. If am able to correlate and differentiate between why things happened the way they did for me, I can understand how they've effected my life then as a child and now as a child within an adult."

    Chaya's tears were saltier this time and she made sure

Chaya's First Death

Kleenex were in arm's reach.

"J' if you could only understand how I am feeling. You may have gone through some things in your life that you are unhappy about and never want to mention again, and this is in no way a competition to see who's childhood or past was the most jacked up, but I know for certain that what has happened to me, did so for a reason. I say that not to boast but had it not been for God keeping my mind, I would have lost it along the way. I just thank Him for that because some folks could not have gone through even half of what I've had to endure and still say that they have their right mind. The way I figure it is He allowed certain things to happen to me that He chose to pass over others and visa versa. He allowed it all not just so I could have a story to tell, but a story to tell that will help somebody else."

~~~~~~~~~~~~~

"Hey Coy! Come here baby and please make sure Beta is up as well. I need y'all to come here for a minute, but not before you take care of the three things!"

Coy shook Beta until she got up. All she ever did was whine Coy thought. But that didn't stop her from reminding her baby sister of their daily routine that had to religiously take place.

"Beta, mamma wants us to come downstairs but not before we brush our teeth, wash our face and...Than..."

"Yeah, yeah, I know...Thank the Lord for waking us up this morning!"

Beta had a smart mouth. In ways, she was a mini version of the adult Chaya. While Coy, looked and acted like the young Chaya, more reserved and to herself.

After little missy finished her prayers, she remembered that today would be a special day.

"Coy", she quietly whispered, "you tell mamma about today?"

"Nooo, what's today?"

Coy could play crazy in a heartbeat like she was in another

A. *Life* Gant

world at times.

From downstairs their mother called them while she was ironing their school clothes. This time she yelled for the youngest first to see if she had complied with the instructions given by her only, older sister.

"Bay'? You up yet?"
"Yeeessss"
"Well y'all come here!"

The sounds of the feet on her children making their way to her, was that of a herd of oxen. The transition from one level of the house to the other was hardly ever a smooth one. The girls would almost always fuss over who would come down first or who was going too fast. Whatever it was, it didn't matter. However, they did not know that they would find their mother ironing her tears out of their clothes.

When Chaya saw her girls, she quickly knelt down to their level and hugged them for what seemed like eternity. The longer she held her babies, the more she began to sob. She cried because she was learning that they were her blessed assignments from God and she would treat them as such. She cried because she loved them and would do anything, including almost everything for them. Who else did she or they have? She cried and she hugged them. She hugged them and then she cried some more. And she prayed...aloud with them in her arms.

"Lord help me."

Sniffling and snorting, she repeated herself.

"Lord help me. Help me be all You've created me to be so I can help them be all You've created them to be. I want to be a better mother than I had and I want them to be better than me too. Maybe You've allowed me to go through some of those things in my youth for my babies and if so, that's alright with me. Who else would I want to go through something for? So...Lord I am askin' for Your favor. Your favor, Your grace and Your mercy, to take me places I have never been before so that I can show them

Chaya's First Death

places that they may never see without me. Use me in whatever way You see fit because You are the example, as a child, I wished I knew I had."

Chaya's daughters were now teared up because although they didn't know why she was crying, they hated to see their mamma cry. At the same time they questioned her tears.

"Mamma, what's wrong?"

When her response was delayed, they gave each other a once over about telling her about today. Beta, at times the bold one, decided she'd be the one to break the fascinating news.

"Mamma, today is picture day and we don't have to wear our uniforms, Mrs. T. said it!"

There it was. Chaya's tears began to flow again. That's the reason for the dream! God was helping her. He was helping her as she'd asked Him to. She desired to be a better mother and here was her chance. She wasn't asleep. She was fully awake. She didn't have to worry about that part but she did have to worry about her own 'Mister'. He would not have any money to give his daughters for pictures. Still Chaya knew this was her chance to change that nightmare into something sweeter. Only it would turn out slightly different.

Where was the money coming from? Oh well, she thought, I have used overdraft protection before for stupid reasons and today was certainly not one of them. Her babies were taking pictures regardless, and she most definitely would make them pretty!

Today was her off day and Chaya had a long list of things she had to do. First, she would balance her checkbook so she would know how much over she went after writing the school a check. Then, she would go to the store to get some cleaning products.

Her house was in definite need of some TLC. Today was the day for general cleaning. Her children were at school and her husband, Josh was going to work. Or was he?

Looking at the clock and him still laying in the bed, she asked him just that.

"Are you not going to work today? Or are you off?"

Before he got a chance to answer, she drilled him the more.

"I thought you went to work on Monday's? Are you using vacation time? Because if you are, have you not considered that maybe we could use it for more important things, like...a real vacation?"

"I thought today was just a good'a day as any."

Joshua had already planned to talk with his wife about the other night when he was thought to have been asleep. That is why he took off but she wouldn't know until later.

At the risk of not ruining her day, Chaya left to run her errands while her 'mister', Mr. Joshua, watched television and lounged in bed.

~~~~~~~~~~~~~~

Chaya came home to a candle lit meal for two. The room was clean and the kitchen floor, swept and mopped. What had gotten into him? She thought maybe he was getting his act together and wanted to help out instead of having a hand out. Who knew, but this kind of change was always a welcomed one.

"J' what is all this? Are we celebrating something that I forgot about?"

Joshua slightly nodded, but didn't.

"You did not forget anything, in fact it was you who made me remember."

Chaya had a puzzled look an her face and just said,

"Okaaay", in questioning manner.

Josh started in as he took the bags from her.

"Well baby, we...are...celebrating me. We are celebrating the new me!"

What has gotten into him? The new him was scaring her a little.

Chaya's First Death

"Baby, I need to make some changes in my life and I kinda knew it but the other night you refreshed my memory. I want to do right but I need your help. I know I have some issues but I can't handle them on my own. Yes, I've prayed but I believe God is wanting me to take some steps first, so here I am. I ask that you pray and stand in agreement with me. You and I both know what I need to do to, so there's no need in going into detail."

The suspense was eating at her and she had to ask him.

"What other night are you talking about and how did I refresh your memory?"

"When you got up to make you some tea, I got up right behind you but you didn't know. I could barely sleep because you were having a bad dream. Anyway, after you finished whatever you were doing in the kitchen, you came back to bed. It was then that you began to pray and talk to my spirit, as you'd put it. The kind of praying that you did that night is the kind I need you to keep doing because like I said, this battle is one I can't handle alone. I must fight it with my other, better half."

"Sooo...you mean to tell me you were awake?"

Chaya was slightly upset because she felt he should have told her. Then again, if he was knowingly awake, she might not have spoke all her feelings, so she decided to just count this as a hidden blessing.

Her husband was making the decision to change for the better, he needed her help and she would do what she could if it meant that her marriage was going to be saved.

"Yes, baby I was awake. Not because I was trying to hear what you were saying but because I couldn't get back to sleep. I apologize if my being awake made you mad but I didn't want to interrupt your time with the Lord. Please Help Me Baby. Would you please help me help myself?"

Her nod made him smile.

Chapter Seventeen

"One-eight-hun-dred-three-two-three-six-seven-six-seven Lord please let somebody tell me where my kids are at."

The ringing lasted for about twenty seconds but to Sadie it lasted a lifetime.

"You have reached the Department of Human Services Child Endangerment Office. If you know your party's exten...."

"Two-two-one-four."

Sadie spoke each number as she dialed it.

"Why did that lady give me the number to the child endangerment office? My kids are not in any danger."

Sadie only wished the former were true.

"C.E.O. How may I help you?"

At the sound of the administrative assistant's voice, she froze and couldn't speak.

"C.E.O. How may I help you?"

"Uh...yes, this is uh...Sadie Edwards and I am supposed to speak to a ...to a...Miss...Thomas. She's got my kids.

"Well hold on ma'am. While I am quite sure that Ms. Thomas doesn't have your children, she might know where they are, seeing that she is the case manager over this department. If you give me sec. I will check and see if she is available and I will put you straight through to her line. You said your name was Sadie?"

"Yes, Sadie. Sadie Edwards."

Chaya's First Death

"Okay Miss Edwards just in case we get disconnected, what is the number where you can be reached?"

Sadie gave the clerk the number and she was patched right to the desk of her case worker.

"This is Miss Thomas, how can I help you?"

By now, Sadie grew tired of answering questions as stupid as her name again and again.

"This Is Sadie and I wanna know where my kids are!"

"Now hold on Miss Edwards, I am not the one you should be mad at. You need to be mad at yourself. This never would have happened if you were home!"

"Who do you think you are talking to? Lady you don't know me. You don't know nothing about me! What happened to my kids and where are they?"

"Miss Edwards your children were found to be in an abusive, unsupervised situation. The oldest girl was sexually assaulted by a man much older than she..."

"What? When?"

"Sadie are you at home now? The problems at hand need to be discussed face to face. I am sending a car for you. Isn't your address...?"

"Yes Ma'am. But why do I need to come there? Why can't I know right now where my kids are? I need to see my kids, Mrs Thomas, I need to see my kids!"

She began to cry and although Mrs. Thomas was a prude, she felt sorry for her client and assured her that if she complied, everything would be alright.

Sadie hung up the phone and cried the more. For some reason, she really didn't believe Mrs. Thomas and fear grabbed her taking complete control.

Just as she was calming herself down, the car came for her and a knock landed on her door.

"Police open up!"

Sadie must have been dreaming.

A. *Life* Gant

"Police open up!"
She had to have been dreaming because she was waiting on a car to come from the C.E.O. Had the case manager lied? People did say she was something else but over the phone was a different story. Mrs. Thomas acted like a ray of sunshine but here she was stabbing me in the back. But why? What did I do?
Why are the police at my door? Do they think I did something to my kids or allowed something terrible to happen to them? God please help me.' Sadie's mind was racing a mile a minute.
"Wh-wh-who is it?"
"It's the Police! Miss Edwards you have five seconds to open this door or we are coming in!"
How'd they know her name? Was she in some trouble that she knew nothing about? She was afraid so at about the fourth second she opened the door just as they were kicking it in.
"Sadie Edwards you are under arrest for child endangerment. You have a right to remain silent..."

~~~~~~~~~~~~~~~

"I want my momma! When is our momma coming for us? Can we call our momma?"
Sadie's girls were tired of being away from home.
"Hello? Hel-lo-o? Is there anybody there?"
The three little women were on their way to a group home but since they put up a fuss, the detective ordered them to sit in a juvenile detention center until they got themselves under control.
The officer on duty was ordered to make sure the girls were okay but not at the expense of them getting on his nerves. They were beginning to do just that. Walking over to the girls holding room, he told them that if they would calm down, he would see what he could do about making a call to their mother. Little did he know that she had been taken to jail, but he would try nevertheless.
"Ladies are you hurting anywhere or do you need to use the restroom?"

Chaya's First Death

> They knew that answering yes to these questions would grant them a short-term release.
>
> The oldest daughter was a mess. She jumped at the sound of the word man. With her sisters needing to relieve themselves more than she, it didn't matter to her that they had weak bladders. Missy just wanted to get out of that room to see all the men officers that were in the building, besides she was only emulating her mother, Sadie, a woman who put men before more important people and things, like her children.
>
> "Yes sir, I need to go and since I'm going to already be out there, can I try and call my momma?"
>
> The on-duty officer nodded at the young woman-to-be and escorted her to the female officer designated to give them bathroom breaks.
>
> While in the restroom, Missy thought about trying to break out of the juvenile center by way of the bathroom window. After she decided that was definitely not a good idea, she washed her hands, left out and asked the female officer if she could call home.
>
> Dialing and redialing her phone number until the line stayed busy, she cried and handed the phone back to the clerk who asked her if she was successful in her attempts.
>
> Missy wiped the tears from her face, so her sisters wouldn't see them and replied, "Nobody answered".

~~~~~~~~~~~~~~~

> Remembering that she was entitled to one, Sadie used her only phone call to call her cheating boyfriend, William.
>
> Her 'right' mind, her 'first' mind, was talking to her every second of every moment about her stupid decision.
>
> "Now why would you call that fool? The man who has cheated on you on several occasions. The sorry punk who has hit you in front of your girls. Don't forget that he's the one who would not help you in your time of true need. You asked him to help you out and take you to the station, but did he?"

A. *Life* Gant

Sadie kept trying to shake her thoughts but the last one pierced her heart like an ice pick.

"Sadie, this is the man that you keep, time after time, putting before the needs of your children."

"Shut-up!" she said to herself and continued to make her call.

"Hello?"

William answered and a recording of a female voice began.

"This is a phone call from..."

"SADIE"

"...an inmate at the Union County Women's Correctional Facility. If you accept, please press one. If you do not, simply hang-up."

As soon as he pushed the button to accept her call, Sadie rushed in without hesitation.

"Will? Will baby, I'm so glad you were home to answer the phone. Can you puh-leeaze, please come and get me from down here? My bail is only five-hundred dollars. Can you do it? For me?"

"Say' you know I ain't got that kinda money on me"

"Remember when I gave you my check card? I got half. I just got paid and when I get out, I have to pay my rent. So if you go to the ATM, by the store, it's in there! Can you? Please?"

"Weeeellll...I guess since it's coming out of your account!"

"Will? You do have half don't you? I told you I only had half. You know I'll pay you back!"

William really didn't care for Sadie and she knew it but because she didn't have an example of how a real man should treat a woman, she made the wrong choices. He was exactly like all the other men she'd dated. TOXIC!

"Alright, alright! Now you said I can go to the ATM machine by the store? Sadie don't have me running around town going to the ATM and you don't have no money in there! Now

~127~

Chaya's First Death

you have it in there right?"

"Yes Will, didn't I tell you I got paid yesterday? It's in there!"

Sadie was getting fed up with his mess and as soon as she got out of jail, William would be history. She just needed him one more time and that was all. What she didn't know was that he was thinking the same thing.

"Don't play with me Sadie! I'll be there in a little bit. By the way, what's yo' pin number again?"

"Okay. You got something to write with? It is one-zero-one-two. And Will...?"

"Yeessss?"

He answered her in an annoyed question-like tone.

"Thanks...for everything." She smiled for a second and then a frown quickly replaced it.

They both hung up the phone and Sadie was escorted back to her holding cell.

~~~~~~~~~~~~~

On his way to the store, William had his mind on something else. He didn't care the least bit about getting Sadie out of jail. The only thing he cared about was getting to the ATM machine and retrieving the cash. Upon arriving at the corner store, the line was long and he looked at the customers like they had a problem, but he waited anyway. He had a plan and it was being carried out without any complication. Will put the card in the machine, followed the prompts instructions and took out the money Sadie told him to. When he completed the transaction, the receipt was issued with her balance. At the sight of that, Sadie's soon-to-be ex-boyfriend, turned around, put her card back in the slot and cleaned her completely out!

Chapter Eighteen

    James went into the bedroom to make the call to his big brother. He thought if he ever needed the Lord to answer a prayer, it was right now. So he sent up a quick one.

    "Lord, Please give my brother a nice heart. One that would make him let me borrow a thousand dollars. In Jesus' name, I pray, Amen."

    The Lord would not make anyone do anything, he apparently hadn't realized that yet. But he would soon find out.

    "Hey John! How are you doing? How's the wife and kids?"

    James' brother knew when his little brother called sounding extra nice, that meant he wanted something.

    "I am fine James. How about yourself? That ole' crazy lady Delta doing alright too?"

    John laughed at his last comment because he really liked Delta. He just never understood why a woman like her would fall for a sorry man like his brother, James.

    "We are all fine man. Listen bro. I have a favor to ask of you?"

    "James I already knew it was something with you. That's how it always is. You only call me if you want something. You don't ever call me just to see how I'm doing or anything like that. Always got your hands stuck out, waiting for somebody to give you something for free, something you ain't got to work for. Huh James? Huh? When is it going to stop?"

    James was used to hearing his brother fuss about his lifestyle. John was a lawyer at a prestigious firm and he had

Chaya's First Death

gotten James several leads to get a great job and career, but he never went to the interviews or any of the meetings, so actually James knew John had every right to fuss. Especially when it came to him calling and asking for money. John wouldn't say as much to his baby brother if the amount of money he called to beg for was a small amount but this time it was unreasonable.

"Listen big bro, I know you mean well and all, but I didn't call you to hear no' sermon on what I do, the way I do it and who I do it to! And I'm sorry for not calling like I should because we are brothers and nothing will ever change that. I just want to know if you can let me borrow some money. If you do, John I promise to pay you back."

"How much this time James? How much?"

"Well...remember I will pay you back."

John became angry at James' beating around the bush.

"James how much do you need this time? And you better be telling me the truth!"

"A thousand dollars John."

"A thousand dollars! What?! I know you didn't just say no thousand dollars!? And why in hell do you need that much money? Is somebody trying to kill you and you need to pay them off? 'Cause that better be the only reason you need that kind of money!"

James couldn't believe his ears. How did John know and if he didn't what a coincidence! Great. Now he had a loop hole. He would say someone was out to kill him. At least that was partially true. Tony wasn't trying to kill him for some money, although he may kill him if he didn't have the money owed to him. This debt was all James' fault. He didn't have to borrow money from a loan shark. Actually, he should not have been gambling in the first place. "Who told you? How did you know my business?"

John was about to hang up on his little brother but he had to know the rest of the story. A story that may mean the end of his brother's natural life.

A. *Life* Gant

"I can't believe you are talking crazy to somebody you are trying to borrow money from! James have you lost your mind? I want to know who is trying to kill you and why? What did you do to whoever that would make them want to kill you?"

"John that's besides the point! Are you or are you not going to help me out? You know I will get you your money back as soon as I get a chance."

"Now James I know you don't want to hear what I have to say, but I am going to say it anyway. You are a grown man and it is time for you to act like it. You can not go around doing what you want to do and expect other people to pay your bills. Now it hurts my heart to do what I am about to do but I have to...James I will not and can not loan you..."

"Click!"

James hung up!

~~~~~~~~~~~~~~~~

The television was on and it was watching James while he sat in his favorite recliner in a stupor. He hadn't told Delta that his brother wasn't going to loan him the money. He decided to wait and tell her that evening over dinner.

Delta was cooking James' favorite meal. Her fried catfish, potatoes and onions, green beans and corn, were to die for. She was getting ready to celebrate. John, James' brother, was loaning him the money and everything was going to be alright.

Before she met James, she had led a simple life. Working to take care of the needs of her children was her priority. Yes, she had a few house parties here and there but she never hurt anybody. Her pride wouldn't let her borrow anything from anyone, and that is way she wanted to keep it because of this very incident. She strongly believed in paybacks so this Tony guy was not wrong in wanting his money but he was wrong for wanting double. Delta was so elated that John was coming through, that she even resorted to telling James that she would even help him pay his brother back, over dinner.

Chaya's First Death

While fixing James' plate, Delta felt the urge to recite *Psalms 91*. She began to pray asking the Lord to help her get it right. It was her mother's favorite and she loved to hear it. Only it was kind of considered by her mother as "the one you say when trouble was coming."

"Lord, I don't know why this one but okay. Just help me out a bit'" The urge was getting stronger by the minute. *"He that dwelleth in the secret place of the Most high shall abide under the shadow of the Almighty..."* Delta could feel her help coming and the scripture become personal. *"...I shall not be afraid of the terror by night, nor will I be afraid of the arrow that flies by day; nor the pestilence that walks in the dark; nor the destruction that wastes at the noonday..."* She got happier at the next recitation of the psalm and focused on not allowing her tears of joy to fall in the potatoes. *"A thousand shall fall at my side, and ten thousand at my right hand; but...I hear ya' Lord...But!...it shall not,...I said it Shall Not!...Come Near Me!...Thank you Lord.* Now James dinner is ready, come in here and get your plate!"

James took his sweet time and drug his feet which made Delta worry. He was usually the first one to the table and the last one to leave.

"What's wrong with you? You got lead in your butt?"

"Delta I'm just tired is all. Food looks great baby."

"Thank you but don't look so down. You acting like somebody has died. Sh** things could be worse. You could be still wondering where that money is coming from and have that man after your a**! So don't put a damper on my night with your sorry a**! I ain't eatin' in here with you!"

Delta picked up her plate and left, heading towards the living room. She was not as mad at his being tired as she was his lying. He knew she knew better than that. One of her life's many purposes was to make sure all knew and never forgot what she hated most; liars and thieves.

"Baby don't be like that. I just have a lot on my mind.

A. *Life* Gant

Please come back to the table so we can eat together."

Delta was getting that feeling again and she was not shaking it this time. "I'm tired too and my leg is starting to ache, so you come in here. Come on in here and tell me what's really going on."

After making himself comfortable in his favorite chair, plate propped up on his pot belly, he opened the line of communication with Delta concerning the money and the debt owed. "Baby, John wouldn't loan me the money. He went on about ..."

Delta's boiling blood had reached her ears, which were about to send up smoke signals like the cartoons, but what she had just heard was no laughing matter and that was only the half of it. "What did you just say to me? I know the hell you did not just say what I think you said. Get to talking! And don't leave nothing and I mean nothing out!"

"John said no. That's all."

"What? That's all? That's all?" Delta forgot that she needed her cane to walk. She got up, snatched the plate of food from his hands, threw it out on the lawn and told him what she'd wanted to for soo long. "Get yo' sh%# and get out!"

James eyes widened to maximum capacity, his face dripped sweat as if it were great drops of blood and he pleaded for her forgiveness.

"Please baby, please! Don't do this I need you! I can't do this alone! What am I supposed to do now? I still owe the man and I have no other means of getting the rest of the money..."

He was on his knees balling uncontrollably and groveling at Delta's feet. She kicked him off her leg as if her were a dog and out of her house for the same reason.

Delta cried for the next day and a half.

Chaya's First Death

Chapter Nineteen

"The kids are off to school. Do you want to go and get something to eat?"

Mister got off easy and Dinah knew it. Her wanna-be tough exterior melted at the sound of his voice and the feel of his touch.

"Huh? You wanna go where?"

"Wherever you wanna go. It's your choice. I figure that's the least I can do since I made you mad." Mister was almost out of the woods completely until he made his last statement. Dinah hadn't forgot in the first place. She just chose to put it into the back part of her mind.

"Yeah you did do that, but we'll talk about it later! I don't wanna go to breakfast because it's almost lunch time. How 'bout we go to Burgundy's. I heard they had good food."

"Okay, sounds good to me. Let me go home and get cleaned up. I'll call you when I am on way."

"Well hurry up! I am hungry."

Dinah had to quickly shower and get her slow self together because she had to make sure every hair was in place before she went anywhere.

After her shower, she tried to call Sadie to check on her again. Dinah missed her best friend's voice and really wanted to talk to her. They had so much catching up to do. She had to tell her about everything that has happened since their last conversation. Dinah's hand shook as she picked up the receiver and continued to do so while she made several connection attempts. Something was definitely wrong with Sadie and she would soon find out. She purposed in her heart that not another day would go by without her talking to her buddy.

Dinah had finished primping in record time. Her stomach growled and she was getting anxious about her lunch date with Mister. But where was he? An hour and a half had already passed and he only stayed about fifteen minutes away.

"Beep, beeep. Beep, beeep!"

Mister was outside honking the horn on his Cadillac SedanDeville. Dinah was going to curse him out because Delta taught them that horns were for whores. She wouldn't even allow her girls to go to the door. She always said that honking meant they had no respect.

"If a man has any respect for you or himself he would come to the door."

Besides, Dinah thought, wasn't he supposed to call first?

When she went down to the car and got in, he complemented her on how great she looked.

"Thank you, but you know better than coming to my house blowing that horn. Don't no whores live here!"

Mister laughed at her and she smiled back at him

The drive to the restaurant was a quiet one. Both had their minds elsewhere. Dinah couldn't help but wonder if this was the start of something new or were the nerves in her stomach advising her different. While Mister mentally designed how he would fake not having his wallet so she'd be responsible for paying for the check.

~~~~~~~~~~~~

"How many?" The mai'tre d' asked.

He looked very pleasant and if his service was as good as his smile was nice, he would get a decent tip.

"Two please."

Chaya's First Death

    Mister looked dapper as usual and he smiled ever so brightly.
    The waiter seated them at a booth dimly lit by candles and adorned with a crisp white linen table cloth. The menu was categorized by the country the food was from.
    Looking at the American side of the portfolio, Mister was the first to make his decision. He chose the lemon-peppered shrimp scampi sampler as his appetizer and a lobster tail and scallop entree' as his main course.
    Dinah loved seafood so she picked the fried catfish and shrimp platter as her entree only. She knew that would be more than enough food for her.
    During dinner, Mister was very talkative. He and Dinah chatted away. They discussed the future of their new life together. Plans of an expected end.
    "Baby go away with me."
    Dinah was surprised and confused to say the least. But what would she say to him? No? Instead she decided to pick his brain a little further.
    "What are you talking about? Go Where?"
    "Go away to Hawaii with me and then on a cruise to the Carribean. What do'ya say?"
    Without hesitation. Dinah screamed acceptance.
    "Yes. Yes. Yes!"
    With a mouthful of lobster, he told her how happy she'd made him. He promised her he would show her the world and Dinah couldn't be happier.
    There was only one thing she forgot.
    Her tears of joy and thoughts of the beach drowned out any worries she had. Even the ones about the welfare of her children. Maybe her mother could take care of them as usual. She pushed that out of her mind for now, mentally saying,
    "Oh well, we'll worry about that later".
    There was absolutely nothing in the world that could put a

A. *Life* Gant

damper on this evening. Dinah and her man would be together now and that is all that mattered.

"Here is your check sir."

"Uh... no Sir. We are going to want some dessert and a bottle of your finest champagne."

While looking at Dinah and smiling, he continued.

"Celebration is in order."

"Wow! What are we celebrating?"

The head waiter was ready to pop the cork at the answer.

"Our new life together. Just me..."

He held her hand and kissed it after every word.

"...and this beautiful woman."

Dinah blushed at Mister's words and was now certain things couldn't get any better than this. After the last toast of champagne and bite of what seemed like an endless slice of pie, the check was discreetly replaced.

"Woe...!"

"What is it? Is something wrong?"

Dinah didn't think he could be talking about the check because they both knew Burgundy's was among the top in fine dining. True enough it was expensive and no wonder, the prices were a' la carte!

"I didn't realize that my lobster tail would be ninety-seven dollars all by itself! Man...! Oh well."

He reached for his wallet and knowingly, on accident, left it back at his apartment.

Mister had taken females to Burgundy's in the past and he knew it was extremely expensive. Besides, he figured having just told her he'd take her around the world and since she hardly ever had her children, she had the funds. He was sure of that. His eyes widened in false disbelief.

"What? What's wrong?"

Dinah's stomach started churning again.

"I-I I think I lost my wallet or either left it back at my

~*137*~

Chaya's First Death

apartment. I was rushing trying to get to my baby."

He gave a sly grin.

"Okaaay? What's that supposed to mean?"

"It means I'ma need you to get this one and I'ma have to pay you back. I am so sorry baby. I didn't mean for this to happen. I promise I will pay you back just as soon as I find out where I put my wallet."

"Hump...You better be glad I just got paid or we'd be up the creek of embarrassment without a paddle. Ooh...I can't believe this."

Dinah was disgusted as she pulled out her billfold.

"Baby, don't be like that. You know I'm good for it. Plus we gotta get ready for our trip this weekend."

"Huh? This weekend?"

Dinah handed the waiter two one hundred dollar bills. She was so excited that she didn't realize the total bill was one-hundred and ninety seven dollars and thirteen cents.

The couple left the restaurant and headed for their new life together, alone.

But how would she tell...or ask her mother if she'd look after Coy and Beta while she left to travel the world with the same guy that Delta overheard grabbed her arm at the club?

A. *Life* Gant

Chapter Twenty

Upon her release, Sadie was issued her belongings and reminded of her court date.

"Now remember Miss Edwards, you are scheduled to be in court on April 18th, 1988 at 9am. You need to have obtained an lawyer for your defense, if you can not afford one, you are free to use the court appointed attorney. Remember you were charged with one count of child endangerment and one count of child neglect. You must prove to the state and the courts that you are the mother you claim to be."

"Yes Ma'am. Thank you for being so nice to me. I didn't mean for any of this to happen. I believe this is my chance to get it right. I think that God has given me a second chance to do things different this time and that is what I am going to do."

Sadie was elated. She was in the process of being released and changed for the better, just as soon as Will arrived.

"Here you are Miss Edwards. Here are your things but first you must sign here showing that you have received your items."

Sadie looked over the document and her puzzled facial expression told the clerk she either didn't understand or she wasn't listening, so the instructions were given again, this time with an addition of advice.

"Right here baby."

The older lady called everyone that was her junior and younger, baby, signifying that what she talked about was usually

Chaya's First Death

something she'd been through, personally or as a direct result from working at the jail.

"Now listen here baby, I don't believe in my heart that what you are going through is by accident. God works in mysterious ways and He'll use whatever way He need's to, to get your attention."

Looking at the clock on the brick wall, the elder continued.

"Who is coming to get you?"

"My boy...well my soon to be ex-boyfriend. He should've been here by now."

"As I was saying, God moves like He wants to move and if you don't take heed the first time, He does drastic stuff the next. Now you know that just because you getting out of this jail, doesn't mean you are free from guilt. It just says you or somebody close to you had a little change for bail. You have to prove to the state that you had no fault in this incident with your baby."

As she was preaching to Sadie, Will walked up and grabbed her belongings out of her hand, a fake attempt to look like a decent man. The lady gave Will a once-over, sensing a bad vibe and continued giving her advice which this time, sounded more like a warning.

"You take care and remember what I said. He works in mysterious ways."

Sadie walked out of the jail house a free woman, physically.

The drive home was tense and she could feel it as if it were a cloak wrapped around her.

"Thanks for coming to get me Will. I appreciate it very much. I don't think I could've stayed overnight in that place. Jail is no place for women, men either for that matter. Giving all your rights to someone else, controlling your every move. Uh uh, nope! It's not for me. Anyway what's up with you? Why are you so quiet?"

To keep from lying and sounding as suspicious as he

A. *Life* Gant

looked, he just resorted to the usual....
"I'm alright, just tired is all. Gotta big day at work tomorrow."
If she didn't know nothing else about this man, Sadie could tell when he was lying, and he was doing just that. But what could he be lying about? What was he trying to hide? She would soon find out but now was the time to call Dinah, her best friend. Too much time had passed and they hadn't spoken in days.

~~~~~~~~~~~~~~~

Arriving home to an empty apartment on a school night would be strange. Sadie almost tripped over the mail that had been pushed through the mail slot on the door. Will saw her stumble and he still clumsily followed suit.
"Here is your stuff. I gotta go home and get some sleep. I will talk to you later."
Kissing her on the cheek, he turned around and left. Slamming the door behind him.
"What is up with him? He is really actin' strange."
Sadie knew he was hiding something now. If it was another woman, she didn't care, because she'd already decided that she was finished with him. Besides, calling her buddy was top priority now.
"Please be home Dee, please be ho...."
"Hello?"
A male voice answered and it startled Sadie.
"H-Hello? Is this Dinah's place? I-I might have the wrong number."
"No... Sadie right? You've got the right one baby. I heard so much about you. I'll go get Dinah for you."
Mister laid the phone down and called for Dinah.
Sadie was speechless. Mister was over there? But who was he, answering her friend's phone? And then having the nerve to call somebody baby? Boy we have a lot of catching up to do. Sadie's mind was going and it would have run further had not her

Chaya's First Death

friend's voice interrupted.

"Saaaayyy! Hey girl! Where have you been? I missed you! What's really going on?"

"Giiirrrl! Where do I start?"

"At the beginning!"

Dinah was anxious to see why her friend hadn't called her in days.

"Okay. Whew!"

Sadie took a deep breath and began.

"Dee remember when we talked the last time and you was fussing at me about taking care of my kids and not leaving them at home by themselves?"

"Yeah and...?"

"Well anyway, something happened to the girls when I went somewhere...."

"What Sadie? What happened to the girls?"

"Dang Dee if you just let me finish! What I was trying to say before I was so rudely interrupted was that something happened when I wasn't at home. The two youngest girls were playing outside, after I told them to stay in until I got back. The baby girl fell off the monkey bars and hurt herself. Not bad though. But anyway, a neighbor who saw the whole thing, was bringing her to me but found Miss Thang, my oldest, having sex with a twenty-one year old man. She called the police on him and they in turn, took my babies. When I got home I noticed they were gone and called around for them but nobody had a clue...."

"So are the girls alright now?"

"Well actually they should be coming home sometime tomorrow. They are in DHS custody. The police said they were in grave danger and needed to be removed from the situation."

"Man Say' I'm sorry to hear that. You alright though?"

"Wait Dee that ain't the half of it. I gets a call from the police department telling me that they had the girls and I should come down there for questioning. I tell them okay and find out, I

A. *Life* Gant

have no gas to make it down there. I called Will and he wouldn't even help, said he was tied up and he would talk to me later. You know I was mad don't you? Anyway, I walked to the store with the gas can and try to hitch a ride back, nobody wanted to help so I walked back home and got attacked by a dog."

"Ha Ha Ha, Ha ha ha! I'm sorry Say' but imagining you running from a dog is hilarious and you know it. Ha ha ha."

"Shut-up. Ha ha ha. It is pretty funny though right now. But when it was happening it wasn't funny at all. An-y-way-s, I made it home too late and they sent the girls with *Mrs. Thomas*.."

Sadie said her name with a slanted attitude.

"This witch doesn't want to give me any information when I call her and lies to me telling me she's sending a car to pick me up because we need to talk in person. Turns out the car that's coming to get me is the police!"

"You lying!"

"No I ain't! After they came to get me, they told me I was under arrest for child endangerment and neglect."

Dinah got quiet just as her buddy finished her last statement, because she kinda always knew Sadie would one day suffer the consequences of leaving her kids at home.

"They took my black a** to jail and I had to call that punk Will to come and get me."

"Well that's sweet. He came to get you out of jail."

"Oh don't go there! He only came to get me with my money."

"What do you mean with your money?"

"Like I said, with my money!"

"How'd he do that Say?"

"Long time ago, I needed him to go to the store for me and I gave him my spare ATM card."

"Say' you didn't?"

"Yes I did and what is that supposed to mean?"

"Have you checked your balance since then?"

~143~

Chaya's First Death

"No but should I?"

"Uhh Yeah!"

"Alright I will as soon as I get off here with you. So he comes and picks me up and ...Oh yeah before I forget, I have to go to court in April...and has the nerve to have an attitude when he drops me off like it was only his money that was spent. Ain't that something?"

"Yeah that's something alright."

Dinah was being sarcastic.

"Enough about me. What's up with you and Mister? You got the man answering your phone now?"

Sadie was tired of talking about herself so she changed the subject directing it towards Dinah.

"No he was just picking it up for me because I was in the bathroom. I told him to and since we had our little spat about the club scene, he has been nothing but nice with the exception of... no I will tell you about that later..."

"No you will tell me about it now!"

"Okay, Okay! We went out to eat..."

"Where?"

"I was getting to that!"

Both friends were just alike. They didn't like the other butting in or telling them what to do. But they did it to one another anyway.

"As I was saying, we went out to eat *At* Burgundy's. Brother man had a gang of food and to make a long story short, when the bill comes he just so happened to have left or lost his wallet somewhere and I had to pay for a two-hundred dollar meal. But he promised to pay me back though."

"What did you say? Y'all doin' like that? Going to a snooty restaurant. But seriously y'all had a two-hundred dollar meal and you treated him?"

"Was you listening at all? I said...forget it you'll never get it!"

A. *Life* Gant

"I heard you cry baby. You said he didn't have his wallet and all that but I was just joking because of the way it sounds. Since that was the case and so it don't sound as bad as it really is, you should just say that you treated Mister to a nice dinner because you ain't never getting that money back!"

"I know you ain't talking!

"Alright. Alright. You right,. You right. Anyway let me get off here. I gotta call my bank to check my balance."

"Hey Say before you get off, guess where I'm going?"

"Where?"

"First to Hawaii then on a Cru-oose!"

"With who? Mister? Hey hey! So is this the payback for the dinner?"

"No! He asked me to go before.....Oh my gosh you think?"

"Could be Dee. Could be. But only a little bit of it because I am definitely sure that the plane tickets alone, cost more than dinner. So look at it that way. You paid for at least half the tickets."

"Yeah that's a way to look at it. But let me go because he is coming out of the bathroom. I'll call ya' later."

"You right, because I still gotta call the bank."

Sadie and Dinah hung up and promised to catch up before Dinah's trip.

~145~

Chaya's First Death

Chapter Twenty-One

"So how will I know if this change is a permanent one? We have been through this "I'm gonna change" scenario, more than once. And I'm not saying it as if you are the only one who needs to change, of course I could stand a few myself..."

Josh annoyingly cleared his throat.

"Whatever! You know what I am saying. I have never intended for you to be the only one who changes but certainly the changes that must take place in you will in turn cause a paradigm shift for the whole family. See what I'm saying?"

"Yeah I know what you mean. All I am saying is that I will need some help. Not the kind that constantly fusses or goes off about any and everything I do. Baby I don't need that."

"J' I hear what you saying but you keep going around the answer to the question I have asked. When will all these changes take place and will they be permanent ones? Are my questions too hard to answer?"

"They are right now. Baby all I can say is give me some time. It is then and only then that I, we can judge rightly. Is that okay with you?"

"Well I guess it's gonna have to do for now. So what's next?"

"What do'ya mean? What's next?"

"I mean what's next for us. For our family?"

"Oh yeah! I'm glad you asked because I was thinking we should go somewhere as a family and take the girls too."

A. *Life* Gant

"Like where J'? Quit beating around the bush."

"I think Kansas is a good place to go. I saw a thing on t.v. about that state being a nice place to visit. It has theme parks and shopping malls and everything and it only costs five hundred dollars for a family of four and the tickets to the parks are included! Soooooo.......what do'ya say? You wanna go?"

Seeing the spark in his eyes, the one she saw when they first met, caused her to accept his proposal.

"Well alright, I guess if you think this is a good idea and a jump start to the new you, my old husband, let's do it!"

The couple hugged and both secretly prayed to themselves that this would be it. There would not be any more arguments or disagreements concerning their family's finances and such. They would lead happy, almost stress-free lives as God intended, maybe.

~~~~~~~~~~~~~

"Are y'all buckled in?"

Joshua tried his best to make sure the family was buckled in safely before each extended trip.

"Yeeeessss."

Coy and Beta competed to see who could answer first and the loudest while they were in the back seat.

"Alright, everybody be quiet and bow your heads." Praying was another item on the list of Josh's routine.

"Dear Lord, thank You for this time You have blessed us to come together and be together as a family. I ask that You keep us safe while we are traveling over the dangerous highways and byways and I thank You right now for our safe return. In Jesus' Name, Amen."

"Mamma looook!"

Beta was extremely excited about being able to go to the amusement park. The last time she had been she was too small to remember.

"Can we have some of that cotton candy? The pink and

Chaya's First Death

blue swirly one? Not that one. But that one over there?"

"Hold on Ma' let's wait and see if there is something else you want. We just got into the park and I am sure you will be beggin' for something else!"

With a sad look on her face, Beta agreed. As if she had a choice not to, she was only five.

Joshua was as big a kid as the girls and his face lit up like a Christmas tree when he saw that the theme park had a race car track as a ride for *bigger* kids.

"Hey baby let's go over here and see how long the line is. I want to ride, well drive one of those cars. You can drive one too and the girls can ride with us. One in your car and one in mine.

Chaya looked at him like he was crazy because he knew she wasn't one to ride on rides. But what her look had in it also was one of disgust. Had Josh not realized that although this was family time, the theme park was for the kids, the real kids, first?

"Babe, I know you excited and all but can we not wait until the girls have had a chance to ride on something? You can't expect them to be happy about being passengers in every car ride can you? After they do what they want to do and get tired doing it, it is then and only then that we, you should have pleasure."

Joshua was not happy at Chaya's last comments but being the easy-going guy that he was, he went along with the plan anyway.

"Daad-dy? Can we have some of that fun-nail, fun-nell, funnel cake over there? I saw a little girl with one and it looked gooood."

Coy was a reader and the words that were not common to her she made sure to sound them out until she got it right.

"When we get back over there to where your mamma is you can ask her, because I don't have any money with me."

"Well if you don't have any money for that funnel cake..."

Coy was a great negotiator as well.

"... how 'bout them dippin' dots? The sign says they cost

only one dot nine five. I think that means one hundred ninety five dollars. Huh daddy?"

Coy's daddy as she liked to call him, laughed at her observations and responded with laughter still in his voice.

"Uh, No baby. I don't think so. That number means one dollar and ninety-five cents."

"Really? Is that all? You don't got that either? *Dang!*"

"Coy watch your mouth."

Joshua smiled from within at his oldest daughter and her mature conversation. But it really hurt his heart because he knew this was a slap in the face. Time had passed long ago that he needed to get his act together and this trip was supposed to be proof of that. The next thing that came to mind after the thoughts of his baby, was that he had put his foot in his mouth about the trip. He knew that he wasn't financially ready to take on the responsibilities of paying for a family vacation, but he would worry about later.

The day was far spent. Coy, Beta, and Chaya, were ready to pass out, but the man of the house was ready to play.

"Okay. Now that the girls are tired of crying and begging, let's go and get on the cars first. That thing over there. And then the water ride. I'll be cool after that. Is that alright baby?"

"I guess J' but can we make it snappy because the girls are whining and I am tired of hearing them. Plus, I ain't spending no more money in this park. We've only been here for a day and a half and we still gotta eat and stuff."

"Hey Beta you can ride with me and Coy you go ride with your mamma."

"J' I don't want to. How 'bout you ride twice and take one at a time?"

That would have been just perfect for Joshua but the girls wanted their parents to race. Reluctantly, Chaya agreed, for their sake.

That evening at the hotel, everyone except Chaya went

Chaya's First Death

swimming. She had forgotten to bring her drawstring ponytail and didn't want to get her hair wet, so she considered this time alone to be a privilege. Using it to relax and read one of her favorite books by Bishop T.D. Jakes, the quiet time was just what she needed. But not before she read her evening scriptures and prayed a bit.

"Well Lord it's just me and You. Forgive me for not giving You praise more than I have. I have just been so consumed with trying to make everybody else happy and in return feeling like crap myself. I don't know how I've lasted this long living like I can take care of people and things with out You. Help me Lord."

Chaya couldn't see the words of her book clearly because she was tearing up at the words of her *talk* with Jesus. She got up to retrieve some tissue to wipe her face. She could hear Him speaking back to her.

"Cast your cares on Me because I care for you. Lean on Me and not on your own understanding, that is your problem. You already know that My ways are higher than yours and My thoughts higher than yours. So you should not feel the need to try and fix everything. That is My job."

At the words of her Heavenly Father, her stress subsided. There was never a need to worry but she still felt the need to. A need to know how the rest of the trip would be paid for when she was out of cash. Would another bill at home have to be sacrificed because of the financial strain? Maybe, but her family would not find out because she wanted them to have fun and she would carry this secret burden alone.

Chapter Twenty-Two

"Tammy, I don't know what's done got into James. I know he's a nice guy and all but I can't deal with no man not taking care of business. He fooled me once. Shame on me. But I'd be da**ed, if he fool me again. But you know something? I miss'em and in some strange way, for some strange reason, I kinda' want him to come back. He can be a good man and maybe it is up to me to help him get better, but he gotta' want to!"

Tammy, one of Delta's best friends, always had a listening ear when it came to her girlfriends needing to talk, but this conversation was one she secretly enjoyed hearing.

"Well Del' you don't need'em if you gotta take care of'em. James was a nice guy but do you think he will get better?"

"Was? You talking about him like he's dead or something!"

"Hump! He will be if he don't get Tony his money! Ha ha ha!"

Tammy was joking and she knew Delta was going to go off on her so she shut up quickly.

"You think that sh** is funny don't you? How in the hell do you know so much? And...how would you feel if Tommy's dumb butt was in some kinda trouble?"

"Del' you gotta lighten up. You always so da** serious! You wanna know how I know? First you must remember that my hus-ban-d was with him when his stupid a** was held up! And furthermore, James came over last night and was begging Tommy

Chaya's First Death

for the money!"

"Now hold on Tammy! You must have forgotten who you are talking to! I will still whoop your a**! I've been trying to hold my tempa' but you pushing it!"

"Del' why you always gotta resort to violence? Always talking about whooping up on somebody. Have You forgotten about that ole' leg of yours? Huh?"

Delta was laughing now because she couldn't believe this 'winch' was talking crazy.

"Tammy shut-up! You and I both know that it doesn't take a good leg to whoop you! I'll tear your a** up with my hands tied behind my back and leaning on my bad leg! Don't mess with me right now, I'm tired!"

"Alright Del' quit tripping and calm down. I can't honestly say that I understand because Tommy ain't never been in no trouble. At least none that I know of. But if he was, I'm sure I would feel the same way as you. So what are you going to do?"

"I don't know but I got this bad feeling and I need to find him for he get into some more trouble."

Just as Delta was speaking, she heard some tires screeching outside in front of her house. By the time she got up, there was already a knock at the door.

"Who is it?"

Tammy was looking as scary as usual. If something was to go down, she definitely was not one to count on.

"It's Tony!"

"Who?"

"Tony!"

Delta gave her friend a puzzled look and instantly her stomach told her something bad had happened to her James.

"What do you want? James ain't here."

"I don't want to talk to James. I wanna talk to you!"

Tony was being belligerent and Delta was ready to curse him out.

~152~

A. *Life* Gant

"What do you want to talk to me about?"
"Ma'am just open the door so I can speak to you face to face."

At his request, Delta put the chain on the door and cracked it.

"Yes? Is there something wrong with James?"
"No Ma'am. I just came by to warn you that James is going to be in a lot of trouble if he doesn't come up with my money."

He glanced at his wristwatch.

"Right now it is a little past eleven, about eleven o' nine to be exact, and I have already told him he better have my money by seven o'clock tonight. If he doesn't I'm coming back over here and I'm taking whatever I want that adds up eighteen hundred dollars you hear me?"

"Now you listen hear ni**a, you ain't coming over here taking a got'da** thang! You hear me? Now I don't know you are and really don't care to either but I wish you would come up over here trying to take me and my kids' stuff! Now I'm going to give you fair warning, if you come back over here and so much as pick up a piece of my trash, you better get ready to meet your maker, because you gone be one dead S.O.B.!"

Delta slammed the door and discreetly rubbed her breast, making sure her gun was still in tact.

"Oh my gosh, Delta what are you going to do? Girl, I gotta go because I do not want to be over here when your crazy but starts shooting at folk!"

"Tam' shut up with your scary a**! You are always whining about something. Don't nobody want you! And since you want to know what I am going to do, I'ma let you in on a little secret that really ain't a secret at all, If that sucka' comes up over here trying to take something that don't belong to him, I'm going to jail! Now move over! I gotta call around to see where James is at, because he'll be a dead one too! HUMPH!!!"

The house was filled with noise but at the same time, it

Chaya's First Death

was silent. Delta was home alone. Tammy had already left. The television was off and all the lights except the living room lamp, were off. The noise was coming from Delta's head and she couldn't stop the thoughts of this morning's meeting, now combining with the thoughts of the evening drama due to take place.

She desperately needed to make some phone calls. The first one was to her other buddy, Sandra, who would give her right arm to Delta if she was a match.

"Hey San' what are you doing? Can you come over here because I sure do need you right now?"

Without hesitation, Sandra snatched her keys off the hook and flew over to Delta's house. As she turned into the driveway she couldn't help but see the tires skid marks that ran the length of Delta's front yard.

"Hey Hun' you okay?"

Delta fell into Sandra's arms from exhaustion and cried.

"Del' what's wrong? You gotta tell me what's wrong!"

She cried the more.

"Alright now you sit down because I see I'm going to have to get my pistol. Del' you better get to talking because I'm going to jail if I find out somebody has hurt you!"

Laughing through the tears at her closest and dearest friend, she motioned for Sandra to sit down.

"Naw Del' you better start 'cause I am going to jail. Better yet, probably the pen. The judge told me if I get in trouble again I'm going to the pen. Now you best give me good reason to go to jail!"

Delta was smiling and wiping her tears while she looked at her crazy friend standing there with her gun in hand.

"San' sit down! I called your crazy a** over here because I needed to talk to somebody other Tammy's scary butt."

"What's up?"

"Girl you remember when I told you about that night I sent

~*154*~

A. *Life* Gant

James and Tommy to the store? And they got held up by a loan shark that James owed some money to?"

"Yeah?"

"Well that punk came up over here talking crazy a little while ago, saying that he was coming back this evening, if James ain't got his money. Of course you know me. I dared him to and I told him I was going to kill him if he did!"

Tears were running down Sandra's cheeks. She laughed hard at her friend imagining the look on her face as she told this man what she was going to do to him.

"Del' I know that's right. Now when He say he supposed to be coming back over here? 'Cause I gotta make sure I am here to set his love right about my partner!"

Delta loved her friend just as much as she loved her. Sandra was that kind of friend that although you didn't talk to her on a daily basis, she was still there ready for whatever, should something go down.

"He said something about seven tonight."

"He? Does 'He' have a name, 'cause if I go to jail I gotta be able to put a name with the face I'm going to blow up!"

At Sandra's last statements, neither of the women could refrain from laughing aloud.

"Tony. Tony is his name."

"Well alright Tony it is."

Sandra smiled, held up an invisible head and repeated it again.

"Tony it is."

"But first I have to find out where James is so I can see if he's alright."

"Oh girl, I just passed him up. He was over Tommy's outside on the porch smoking a cigarette."

"I'ma kick Tammy's a**, she knew I was looking for James. She was just over here and she heard me talking about me having to find him. Let me call over there and see what's going

~155~

Chaya's First Death

on?"
Ring ring Ring, Ring ring Ring!
"Hello?"
A female voice answered and Delta knew who it was.
"Tammy you winch! Why didn't you call me and tell me James was over there? You knew I was looking for him!"
"Del' calm down! He just got over here."
"Tammy quit lying! Sandra came over here right after you left and she saw him on her way to my house, sitting on your porch!"
"Nuh Unh!"
"Whatever! Shut your lying a** up and put him on the phone!"
Tammy put the phone down but it seemed like she threw it down by the way it sounded.
"James? Ja-ames?"
"Yeah?"
"Delta's on the pho-one!"
"Who?"
"Delta!"
Delta was holding the receiver in disgust, thinking, "No he ain't acting like he don't know who I am."
"Hello?"
"James?"
"Hey baby"
"You got a minute?"
"Yeah. What's up?"
"We-ell since you asked, Tony came ove...."
James broke in and had already began to get upset at the sound of Tony's name.
"He what? I'm on my way!"
James slammed the phone down and would have ran home but Tommy offered to take him and did.

~156~

A. *Life* Gant

~~~~~~~~~~~

Back at the house, Sandra and Delta were chatting away discussing their guns and how long it would take James to get there on foot.

"I bet it take him thirty minutes. You know your man is old!"

Delta jokingly frowned at Sandra. "He might be old but he ain't that old. It's going to take him all of fifteen minutes. Probably less than that!" By now, twelve minutes had passed since she talked to him and soon after, the door opened. It had taken James fourteen minutes to get there. Delta looked at Sandra. "I told you!"

"Well I'll let you two love birds catch up and Delta you better call me because I will go to jail if I need to!" Sandra smiled, gave her friend a hug, slapped James on the arm and left.

"So babe, what's going on? You said something about that punk coming over here? What did he say?"

"...Something about coming over here taking stuff if you don't pay him back by seven o'clock tonight!"

"Let me get this sh** straight! He came over here? Over to this house?"

"You think I would be lying about some sh** like that? Yes he came over..."

"Hold on. Don't say another word. I need to go use the bathroom first. My nerves got my bladder all messed up! Hold on baby."

Tommy sat there witnessing the whole thing. He just stared at Delta admiring her beauty and caught himself before she did. Since he didn't like seeing the woman he preferred to be with, in a sad state, he tried to calm her down by telling her he'd give her man the money, on her behalf.

Whispering through the tears, her eyes widened at his generosity. "Really you'd do that for me?"

Chaya's First Death

"Honestly? I'd do anything for you. I'll just tell James I'll help him out and he can pay me back a little something every pay check 'til he gets it paid off. How's that sound?"

James was finishing up in the restroom and on his way out he overheard his woman and his friend whispering as if trying to hide something. Without jumping to conclusions, he interjected.

"How's what sound?"

"Oh, I was just telling Del' I was going to loan you the cash and that you could pay me back when you got paid."

This was the first James had heard about Tommy loaning him the money. Earlier, when he'd asked him, he said he would think about it.

"You serious Man? That is great! I promise I will pay you back as soon as I get paid! Man thank you soo much! I don't know what I'd do without you!"

By now the clock read *6:35pm* and James had to call Tony to tell him he had the money, but Tony broke his promise. The promise that said he'd be waiting on James to contact him and he wouldn't be at the house until after seven. He lied and was spotted camping out in the vacant corner lot two blocks over, well before seven.

When James got the news of his whereabouts, he was on his way to the site but found it empty. In the near distance, he could hear gunshots and immediately ran back towards Delta's house.

"Huh woo! Huh woo! Huh woo!"

James sprinted as fast as his brittle bones would take him. He then began to pray.

"Lord, if I never ask You for anything else, please let Delta be okay. She don't deserve to be in any mess like this!...Huh woo! Huh woo!"

The house was a only a couple streets over and it seemed like he was in a race to win his first *5k*, with no training at all!

"Pop, pop,pop!" The gun sounded more like a canon ball

~*158*~

A. *Life* Gant

than a shotgun.

Delta was ready. She saw Tony's car coming in the distance when she peeked outside to check if the mailman had run. Tommy was still there and Sandra had showed up ready as well. Neither person in her company understood why she was moving so fast towards her purse. Delta had put her pistol there earlier while talking to Sandra. When she emerged with her weapon and found Tony, the loan shark, on her lawn latching a towing chain to her 88 Olds', she opened fire like she had been frequenting target practice. "Remember what I said sucka? Huh? You remember what I said?" *Pow! Pow!* "I told you not to come up over here trying to take my stuff!" *Pow! Pow!* "This sh** belong to me!" *Pow! Pow!*

By now, Tony, who was yelling and screaming obscenities, was trying his best to get out of the line of fire. He had heard Delta was a bad a** chick, but not like this.

"Hey man? Why ain't y'all shooting back at her? Y'all know I ain't packing and y'all 'spose to have my back!" He was hollering at his boys, the same ones who helped him hold James and Tommy up at the convenience store. They just stared in awe at this real-live Charlie's Angel, and couldn't help but laugh to themselves.

"Sh** she shooting at you. Not us!"

"What?" Tony would've shot them if he had his piece on him.

Meanwhile, Delta was still unloading her gun on Tony. One moment she was as close as his head, the next, she'd miss him by a yard. She didn't care. She was just making good on her promise. She promised him if he came up over her house, she was sending him to meet his maker. And she would've done just that, had she not ran out of bullets. "*Sh**! Sh**! Sh**!* I'm out of bullets!

When they heard her say that and by the time she'd finished reloading, James had jumped on Tony's back and started

Chaya's First Death

to fight. Sandra and Tommy had the other two surrounded.

"This is between the two of them. Right?" Tommy was much larger than the two men put together, so they agreed, willingly. If they hadn't, Sandra had her gun already drawn, to make sure that they complied.

"Punk, you ain't nothing without your boys and a gun are you?" *Punch!* "I told you I would have your money!" *Punch!* "Now here it is!"

After getting in a few licks and cursing his debtor out, James handed him the money and walked off. Evidently James was not a fighter because he was never told not to turn his back on an opponent.

"You stupid Ni**a! You think I was just going to sit there and let you unload on me?" *Punch, punch, punch!* "You must have lost yo' gotda** mind! Have you forgot who you were dealing with?" *Punch, punch, punch!* "Don't...ever..." *Punch!* "...ever..." *Punch!* "...come to me..." *Punch! Punch! Punch!* "...again for nothin'..." *Punch!* "...else..."*Kick!* "You hear me?" Tony beat the mess out of James and would've killed him had Delta not reloaded and shot him in the butt and the leg.

All the neighbor's were standing on their lawns watching the whole thing. Not one of them tried to help Delta and her buddies. They were just enjoying the show.

Blood sprayed sporadically on the driveway and in the grass. The grand finale involved the police. Sirens were heard from afar and as they got closer, it was inevitable who they were coming for. Three cars pulled up, each at a different angle. Jumping out of their cars, guns drawn, they instructed everyone to get on the ground. After the witnesses were questioned, four people were handcuffed, including Delta. When no one resisted arrest, the Miranda rights were recited to each of them, all at once.

"You all have the right to remain silent...."

A. *Life* Gant

Chapter Twenty-Three

"Baby, I am so glad we came on this trip. I needed a vacation."

Dinah was in heaven. She had never seen the ocean or been out of the country for that matter.

"Yeah, me too."

Mister was a man of few words and now, even less. Unlike Dinah, who wanted to talk about everything, from the flight there to the beauty of the beach. His silence caused her to dismiss her feelings. "I'll just let'em relax."

The breeze from the ocean cooled off their hot skin while they bathed in the shade.

~~~~~~~~~~~~~

Back home, at Delta's house, the kids were having a blast. Their grandma was out of jail and she threw herself a party. Everyone was invited. She cooked her infamous spaghetti and fried chicken, knowing that the two would spread amongst her family and friends, and have enough for left-overs the next day. The music was great and everybody was having fun.

On her way from the kitchen, Delta slid Tommy the money James owed him. Both giving one another the "it's our little secret" look. Tammy and Sandra, unaware, across the room, sat in their usual places, cheering their "niece" on. Rocking from side to side, Delta sat down to enjoy the entertainment her baby girl offered, by way of dance.

Chaya's First Death

James limped over to where she was sitting and hugged Delta. He was so happy to see her holding up so well. After all that had happened, he was lucky to even be in her presence. She still loved him even though she tried not to. Her heart wouldn't allow her to give up on her man. But for some strange reason, during the last couple of days, she could hear an unfamiliar word ringing in her ears, *Enabler*.

Was God trying to tell her something? Maybe. She would soon find out. But until then, she would wait on Him.

"Party over here!"

James said, tightly holding on to Delta, while Tammy snapped a shot of the two, once again, love birds.

~~~~~~~~~~~~~~~

"Dinah why do you keep pacing the sandy beach? Is something wrong?"

Mister hated the focus being taken off of him.

"I don't know. I just can't shake this feeling I keep getting about my mama. Something is definitely wrong and when we get back to the hotel, I'm going to call home to check up on her and the girls."

"Well if you say so, I thought this was supposed to be our time and nobody else's?"

Dinah had allowed Mister to be selfish for so long, that now, it was getting to her. How could a man who said he loved kids in the beginning, turn out to never want to be around them? And without noticing that her thoughts were overheard, she said, "But my kids aren't bad."

With a look of concern on his face, he asked her what she meant and why she had said what she said.

"What was that supposed to mean? I said nothing about your kids being bad. Did I?"

"No. It was nothing. Don't worry about it."

"What do you mean don't worry about it?"

"I meant just what I said. Don't worry about it. I was

A. *Life* Gant

thinking out loud and you weren't supposed to hear that."

"Baby let's not fuss over spilled milk. This trip is meant for relaxing only and nothing else. You hear me? Nothing else."

Dinah knew he was talking about her shutting up. Lately all she could think and talk about was her family. The Lord was waking her up again in the middle of the night with dreams about something happening if she didn't get her act together. She had already lost the trust of her mother and her siblings and was now losing that same battle with her children. They really loved their momma but now, were beginning not to care if she came back to get them or not. All they knew was that momma was on vacation with her boyfriend. Having fun without them. And although they missed her terribly, they grew accustomed to staying with their grandma, their new Mama.

The room was clean and it smelled good. The housekeeper had come and gone unnoticed. The bed was made and everything looked as if it came straight out of a magazine.

"Look baby, they even hung up all of your clothes that you layed out on the bed."

Dinah was a diva and she had to live up to that reputation, even overseas.

"That's good, where's the phone?"

"Oh, I told them we were getting bad reception and static was the only thing that could be heard. So they took it down to be replaced with a different one. They said as soon as they could, they would bring us another one."

Mister lied through his teeth and Dinah knew it.

"That's okay," she said in a nice voice. "I'll just go downstairs to the lobby and make the call."

"Do you have to go now? Awe..I'm going to miss you baby."

She was not amused with his whining.

"Okay, see ya in a minute!"

~163~

Chaya's First Death

Dinah left that room and began to feel the Lord tugging at her heart. That's probably what He wanted. He allowed that butt hole Mister, to act as a deterrent just to get some alone time with her. When those thoughts subsided, a song flooded her soul and overflowed, spilling out of her lips:

"Yes Lord...Yes Lord...from the bottom of my heart, to the depths of my so-oul...Yes Lord...Com-plete-ly Yeeesss...my so-oul says, Yeess."

"Excuse me Ma'am? Do you have a phone I can use to call home?"

"Yes I do sweetheart and where might home be?"

"Oklahoma. I gotta call home to check on my mother and my kids."

The hotel clerk came back with a cordless phone. Dinah had favor. Usually the guests were instructed to use the phone in the lobby, which of course allotted them only three minutes. But she was given the actual hotel phone and it wouldn't even be charged to their room.

"Hello?"

"Hey Dee Dee, what's goin' on and where's Mama?"

"If you would have been here you would've known that Mama's been to jail and everything."

Dinah wanted to slap her baby sister because she had a smart mouth. She was actually just like her big sister. Thus the reason for their spats, they were too much alike.

"What? I knew something was wrong. Put Mama on the phone!"

"Hello?"

"Mama? What's going on? Is Dee Dee lying? I mean storying...?"

Delta believed that the 'L' word was considered to be cussing. And she didn't care how old her children were or would become. Cussing was always disrespectful.

"...about you going to jail? Where are my kids and where

A. *Life* Gant

were they?"

"Now Dinah did you forget I didn't sleep with you last night?"

"Oh sorry Mama. Good afternoon. How are you doing?"

"I'm doing fine. But before you get to asking twenty-one questions, you better check yourself. Your chil-dren are fine. They were with your sister, Dana, when all this went down. I did go to jail because...."

Delta told Dinah everything. After she told Dinah about the weekend's incidents, she began her motherly speech, telling her daughter what she wished somebody would've told her.

"Now baby, I want you to hear me and hear me well. I realize that some of the things you are doing are a direct result of your upbringing, that is why I fuss so much. I want every last one of my kids to be better than I am. To do better than I have...."

Dinah's heart melted at the sincere words of her mother and Delta knew that this talk was just what her child needed at that very moment. The hotel clerk handed Dinah some tissue and left so she could have some privacy.

"...Dinah Marie you are a blessed child and you know it. Please treat yourself and your children as such. They do not deserve to be pushed aside for the sake of some man who doesn't give a da** about them or you, because if he did, he would know that you all come as a package. Quit making it easy for them men to not treat you and your children like the queens you are...."

Delta heard her daughter's sobs on the other end of the phone and her heart ached.

"...Now Dinah I want you to remember this if you don't remember nothing else, you are better than your surroundings and you were put on this earth to be just that, better...."

"I know Mama...but...."

"No. Don't Mama me! I've been there and done that. I wanted to run around and have fun like you call yourself doing, but I couldn't. I didn't have nobody to take care of y'all while I did

Chaya's First Death

what pleased me, because my mother wasn't having it. And Dinah because of that, I chose to help y'all out as much as possible. Now that don't make me no saint. It was just a choice God allowed me to make and He has helped me thus far...."

"Mama I know what you have done for me. And you may never know how much I appreciate you for it. But I want you to know that I love you and thank you very much...and"

"Dinah Marie, don't keep interrupting me. Okay?"

"Yes Ma'am."

"Dinah I was sitting here and I could hear the voice of God repeatedly saying this word to me. Have you ever heard the word *Enable*?"

Dinah's eyes widened. She had heard the same thing.

"You know it means making something easy for somebody else? That's what I have been doing with James. Doing with you and everybody else. And it's time out for that. Nobody deserves to be used. But what's so funny is in some strange kinda way, I think, well I thought, that being this way was the right way to be. Baby I believe that we, as women in our family, have this strange need to be needed. And if you don't stop doing what you are doing, your kids will one day grow up and do the same thing. You understand me Dinah? You gotta get yourself together. If you don't do it for you, then do it for your kids. They deserve better."

Tears began to flow down Delta's cheeks and Chaya ran to get her some tissue.

"Mama? You aw'right? What's wrong?"

Chaya was concerned and because she overheard her momma crying on the other end, she cried as well, but Delta consoled her.

"Mama is that my baby?"

"Yes. You wanna speak to her?"

"Umm...Yeah."

Delta handed her granddaughter the phone.

"Here. It's your momma."

"Hello? Hi momma..."

Dinah couldn't help herself. She cried tears of pain at the sound of her daughter's voice.

"Momma? You aw'right?"

"Yeah baby, momma's alright. How have you all been doing?"

"Good."

"Y'all having fun and staying out of granny's way?"

"Yeeesss."

"I miss y'all."

"We miss you too momma."

"As soon as I get home we are going to have some fun, okay?"

"Some fun? Like what kinda' fun? Where we gone go? Will we be by ourself? Just you, me and Daya? And can brother come too?"

Dinah knew that Chaya was the stubborn one when it came to coming around to people. She didn't care for Mister and really wished her mother would stop dating him. But Dinah had more 'important' things on her mind besides what Chaya thought about her boyfriends.

"Well we'll see okay?"

To Chaya, that meant Mister was coming and she no longer wanted to talk to her momma. Instead she quickly ended her portion of the conversation and waved at Daya, telling her to come get the phone.

"Okay momma you wanna talk to Daya?"

"Chaya I'll call bac...."

Before she could finish telling Chaya she would call back later, Daya jumped on the phone.

"Hi momma!"

"Hey Day'. Whatcha' doin'?"

"Nothin...we just...and...."

Daya talked her mother's ears off. Dinah smiled at the

~167~

Chaya's First Death

sound of her voice, but she really hoped that Delta would hurry them off the phone for some reason. Any reason. It didn't matter to her. She finally did. About ten minutes to eternity. Dinah hung up and thanked the clerk for her kindness.

"You are quite welcome. Anytime."

On the way back up to the room, Delta's words resonated in her spirit and that word, enabler, was ringing strong. Dinah wondered how her mother knew that she was ready for a change. She didn't say anything. She kept it all inside with the exception of a few words here and there tossed at Mister. "Am I really making it easy for him not to love me like I deserve to be loved? Is it really true that the only time he wants to be with me is when the kids are not around? But he said he loved kids when I first met him." Dinah shrugged her shoulders in an "I don't know" fashion at the thoughts she was having. She reached the door to their room and began to turn the knob but quickly stopped. A feeling came over her to pray and that is what she did, but it wasn't a sincere one. Figuring any prayer was good enough, even the short one she'd just sent up, Dinah opened the door and found Mister on the phone, he said was so broken. He was telling one of his friends how she was clueless to his whispering sweet nothings in some broad's ear. He hadn't even heard her come in. She stood there and listened to his conniving self tell his friend about the woman he'd left with at the club. Apparently, because she didn't have any children, he'd much rather be with her and according to Mister,

"Dinah does have it goin' on, but she got them kids and I don't know how long I can keep her away from the little cry babies. Lady Luck just don't do it for me like Dinah, but I'll see man. I'll see who cracks first. It's gone either be her wanting her kids or giving them to her mama. Or, it's gone be me leaving her because they are around all the time...."

The heart in Dinah's chest beat loud enough for the world to hear it. Everybody, except Mister. It's function just resigned to

A. *Life* Gant

being the bell at a boxing ring. Dinah quietly picked up the lamp next to the vanity and without hesitation or reservation she sprinted the short distance to where he was sitting and...

CRACK!

Dinah knocked him over the head with it and looked to see if he was going to get back up. If he had she would've hit him again. She made known her decision and his, by her next statements.

"That's who cracked first ni**a! This da** lamp over your head!"

Dinah went smooth off! She tried to kill Mister! She told him she would. She remembered her own words if he didn't.

"...about mine...I'll kill you..."

Dinah was mad and the whole hotel knew it. If it weren't for her cursing him out, she would have finished him off. But the same lady who gave her phone privileges earlier, had to be the one to pull her off Mister.

"Baby, he ain't worth it! He ain't worth it!"

"Naw he can't be talking about my kids and disrespecting me! Naw! And to think, I had the nerve to believe he really wanted to be with me?"

Dinah was crying a different kind of tears. They flowed. Not because he did her wrong but because she feared that because of a foolish man, she may have ruined her relationship with her daughters.

While the sweet lady held her, Dinah secretly prayed that God would grant her this one wish if any at all, that He'd bring restoration to her family.

"Excuse me miss? Are you a...uh. Dinah Mary.? Uh... Oh! Dinah Marie?"

The security guard was instructed to call the police. The one who arrived, barely got her name right. Even after looking at the piece of paper in his hand.

"Yes. And who wants to know?"

Chaya's First Death

"Ma'am there has been a report made about some loud noises, commotion, and possibly some violence, coming from this room."

Before she could speak, Mister made a sound and tried to get up, but couldn't. Blood was all over the front of his linen short set. Running down the side of his face. From the top of his head. The police wasn't aware of this part of the situation and arrested Dinah on the spot, taking her to the Hawaii police station.

God was there all the time. She would find out and so would everybody else.

"Ma'am? Now you want to tell us what happened back at the hotel?

"Yes Sir."

Dinah told the Chief of Police how Mister used her and her body. Mistreated her trust and her children. And on top of it all, he was cheating on her, behind her back, in front of her face.

"Well I see. I believe you've got good reason but that doesn't make it right..."

"Yes Sir, I understand."

"...And since the gentleman doesn't want to press charges here in the state of Hawaii, we got to let you go. Now that don't mean he can't do so, in your town. He can make it like it all happened there and we can't say a thing because it'll be out of our jurisdiction. You understand what I'm telling you?"

The only words coming out of Dinah's mouth was, "Yes Sir," and "I understand."

Dinah was dismissed. As she headed for the door, a soft tug on her arm, quickly halted her. She turned around and the Sumo-wrestler-looking officer, told her to take care of herself and stay out of trouble. And that is what she vowed. To him. To God. And to herself.

Dinah wondered how she was going to get home. She didn't know how Mister would act towards her since she bashed his head open. He had the plane tickets in his possession.

A. *Life* Gant

Arriving back at the hotel via police cruiser, she retrieved her things and was surprised to see Mister all stitched up, ready to go, and acting nice! He even helped her pack her belongings to the elevator and put them in the cab.

"Why was he being so kind? Is it because he knew he deserved it?"

Dinah was almost afraid to leave with this man, but at the risk of not seeing her babies, she did anyway.

The plane ride was uneventful. Dinah did her crossword puzzles, while Mister rested his eyes, until they landed.

Both passengers identified their baggage, got in separate cabs and didn't hear from each other again.

Until a couple of months later...a knock was heard at Dinah's door.

"Who is it?"

She peeked through the chain on her door.

"Are you Miss Dinah Marie..."

"Yes?"

She had just been served with court papers. Her court date was April 18th, 1988.

Chaya's First Death

Chapter Twenty-Four

"Ring! Ring!"

"You have reached Union County Credit Union's Automated Banking Center. Please press One if you want to continue in English..."

"Beep!"

"For checking account information press...."

"Beep!"

Sadie knew the prompts by heart and wished there was a way she could run straight through them without having to listen to the robotic computer voice. She wished that a live person was on the other end of the phone, but the bank didn't open until nine in the morning.

"Please enter your checking account number followed by the pound sign."

Speaking every number aloud while she pressed each button, Sadie made sure to do as commanded.

"One. One. One. Three. Pound."

"Please enter your passwo...."

"Beep. Beep. Beep. Pound."

"You have zee-row doll-ars And seven-teen cents remaining."

"What!"

Sadie was hysterical! She hung up and redialed the number repeating the prompts, but this time she went much slower.

"You have zee-row doll-ars and seven-teen cents

A. *Life* Gant

remaining."

"Lord what am I going to do?" She cried. She cried for the next several hours. She cried for the next several hours not so much because of the money, but because she was stuck between a rock and a hard place. Her rent was due and since she didn't have the money, she would be put out! "No Lord please tell me I'm dreaming. This must be a nightmare. Lord Please! My babies will be coming home on a temporary basis and will be taken from me permanently if I don't have a stable place to stay, a roof over my head. Lord please tell me why."

Sadie was not raised in church. She didn't really know much of anything about praying and how God worked, but she remembered Dinah saying something about Him telling her to cast her cares on Him, because He cared for her. So that is exactly what she did, but not before she asked Him to forgive her of her sins.

"Lord I know You may not know who I am and I certainly know very little about You. Wait a minute. Now ain't that stupid! You know everything! Let me start over. Lord you know who I am more than I know myself. So before I start asking You to do something for me I am going to do something for You. Ain't that how You work? I do something and then You move? I think I heard Ms. Delta say that before so...here goes. Lord thank you for the sun, the moon, and the stars and all the stuff You created. You are the one that knows everything. You know what happened to me as a child and why. You also know what happened to my own children. I wasn't there Lord but help me be a better mother than what I had."

The front of her light gray t-shirt, was now dark gray, from her tears and for some reason she switched tunes on her prayer.

"Lord, please forgive me of my sins. I want to do right so help me to do what makes You happy..."

Sadie was weeping more now, but the tears were of joy. She had never felt so at peace in a long time. Commencing to get

Chaya's First Death

up, she remembered she had not asked him about her bills. So she quickly bowed her head once more.

"Oh yeah and Lord, could You help me find a way out of this situation please. I don't have my rent and bill money and I don't know what I can do so I am casting this one on You too, okay? Thank You Lord, Amen."

Her attempts to contact Will failed miserably. She knew he did it. And that coward didn't even have the nerve to face her. But for some reason, she felt alright. She didn't worry anymore about it because Will would get what was coming to him. And God would take care of her. Besides, she had to get her house in order. Her girls were coming home and she would be watched like a hawk for the next two weeks, until her court date.

Sadie went into the linen closet, located in the hallway, and got out her cleaning supplies. The mop bucket was under the kitchen sink. After rinsing it out, she set it aside for later use. But first, she had to clean the rest of the apartment.

"Let me put on some good cleaning music!"

Sadie be bopped over to her stereo, scanned her tape collection and found one she'd never listened to.

"Maybe this is...Yeah, this is the one Dinah gave me. Let's see what's on it!"

"Show up! Somebody ought'a be a witness...Show up!...He will come through for you...He will show up!"

Sadie smiled. God knew what she needed and He answered her through the voice of John P. Kee.

Clapping her hands and stumbling through the words of a song she had never heard, Sadie got happy at the main phrase and repeated it...over and over again.

"He will Show Up!....

Chapter Twenty-Five

    For weeks the house was silent. Coy and Beta even sensed the tension, but remained in a "child's place," continuing on as normal. Only life, for the whole family, was far from normal. Their mamma and daddy didn't say much to each other and when they did, it was anything but nice. However, they did make sure their children were out of site when hell broke loose. A change had to be made.

    Chaya was fed up with the way things had been going at home and so was Josh. They decided that some time apart would be better for the both of them. The girls would not like it but they would get used to it. And if everything worked out as planned, they would all be one big, happy family, again.

    "Well J' I'm tired and you know I have every right to be. I think it is time we both see what we are made of."

    "Chaya you act like I'm not tired. I have to deal with this situation as much as you do."

    "How so Josh?"

    "I have to deal with your attitude and your mood swings because of any ole' thang. You go off at the least little thing."

    "Well you know what Mr. Joshua? Since there is no reason to yell anymore, I will speak to you in a civilized manner. Yes, I have had a smart mouth at times. And I am not saying that that was okay, but you have to remember that it was when you failed me and your kids."

    "What? How did I fail you?"

Chaya's First Death

"Oh don't get me started, Mr. *Assistant* Chaplain! You cared more about the folk at your stupid job, then you did your own family. Brother so and so needs this and sister so and so needs that! I can't compete J'! Weeee, can't compete!"

"I've never asked you to compete, just support!"

"Support?! Support?! You wanna talk about support? Huh J'? What about when we need you here at home? We may need something small done around the house but because it is just that! Small! You put us off to take care of your chaplain duties! For real J?! For real?!"

"Whatever! You are lying and you know it!"

"You wanna bet?"

Joshua knew that Chaya was right to have the feelings she was having but he was hurt too. Instead of going there with her any further, he left, just as he always did. Chaya and the girls saw him on rare occasions. True enough he was a great dad but a poor husband.

Thinking about all that had occurred over the course of their marriage, she cried to herself. "But he said that he would do better." Chaya cried herself to sleep night after night, barely getting any rest and she could hear the Lord saying to her again, *"Come unto Me, All ye that labor and are heavy laden and I will give you rest."* When she let that soak in, her rest and her sleep was good until one morning, not long after the separation, a tap was heard at the door and she was served with divorce papers. She began to tear up and she heard Him speak once again, the same thing, but this time He continued. *"...take my yoke upon you and learn of me...for my yoke is easy and my burden is light..."* Chaya wiped the tears from her face and read the decree which stated she had to be in court on her birthday, April 18th, 2007!

"Well Lord do what you wanna do and be glorified while you do it!" Chaya was able to say this because God had not only given her peace but He gave her the understanding which brought that same peace!

A. *Life* Gant

Chapter Twenty-Six

Chaya's nightmares were becoming so common that she went to bed waiting on them. Now she believed that God gave her answers to most all her questions, this way. Lately, her nights revealed truths about her days and she could feel the climax of everything coming to surface.

"All rise! The honorable Judge, Aycee Porter, presiding. Please come to order."
Judge Porter came in, sat down on her bench as usual, and instructed the courtroom to follow suit.
"Bailiff, have the witnesses been sworn in?"
"Yes Ma'am."
"All those included in the case concerning Mister Jenkins versus Dinah Smith, please come forward."

Chaya turned over on her side. Her sleep could not be disturbed. She must find out why God took her to her mother's day in court.

Dinah and her lawyer stepped forward. Mister's attorney did so as well.
"Council, how do you plead?"
Mister's lawyer was alone, on behalf of his client.
"Ma'am my client is running a bit late but he pleads not guilty."

Chaya's First Death

She looked at the defense on Dinah's side. "Council? And you? How do you plead?"

"Judge Porter, my client is not guilty and pleads as so."

"Mr. Atkins, please keep it simple and let me do the judging. We'll see if your client is as she says she is, but until then, give me only the information I need. Is that clear?" The Judge was known to be as stubborn as a bull when it was needed, but she also wore her heart on her sleeve. In the past she could be seen crying while giving a closing statement and this case wouldn't be any different. "A hearing will be held today at noon. Next case Bailiff?" He handed her the files. "All those included in the case concerning Tony Marelli versus Delta Smith, Please step forward."

Delta had the same lawyer as Dinah. Of course she would because it was James' brother, John, he was like her brother-in-law.

Giving John a look of concern, Judge Porter wondered if he was in over his head. Two cases of this caliber, on the same day, for a new lawyer, was unheard of. "Council, how does the client plead?"

"Ma'am, my client pleads not guilty."

"Very well council, so your cases are not spread out, I'll do you a favor and set this one for one o'clock this afternoon."

"All those included in the case concerning...."

Two hours had passed and next was momma's buddy.

"Sadie Edwards please step forward."

Aunt Sadie, momma's best friend was on trial for child endangerment and neglect, but her case was bogus. Although she could've been a better mother, she was basically having to defend the fact, that, like most, she had a hot-tailed daughter, who needed some home training and a good ol'fashioned butt-whoopin. Uncle John was her defense lawyer too.

~178~

A. *Life* Gant

The Judge that was supposed to handle Sadie's case, was unavailable for an unspecified reason. Judge Porter would fill in, because she was thinking of overseeing family law. This would be one of her first cases and she did not know what lied ahead. The Judge set the time of her trial to begin last. At two-thirty in the afternoon. It appeared to be the most difficult, and she was certain of some complications arising.

Tossing and turning all night, Chaya thought this dream would never end, but God switched it up. He kept the setting in the courthouse but this time she was the defendant. She already knew her court date was soon to come, but maybe the Almighty was showing her the outcome in advance. She was dreaming and daydreaming at the same time!
At this point in the dream God kept Chaya still. That way she could see His salvation at work.

The courtroom drama seemed endless and mundane, but Chaya sat on the bench outside the room at peace, but in pain. Her mind couldn't help but wonder why God had brought all the painful past to her just as painful present. Was he trying to show her the end result to the road often traveled? Maybe. Was he giving her a peek into the lives of folk who leaned on Him only when they needed Him to get them out of trouble? Maybe. Chaya wrecked her brain trying to figure out the ways of God, but he quickly reminded her of the book of Isaiah chapter 55 verses 8 through 9 where it states: *For My thoughts are not your thoughts, Nor are your ways My ways says the Lord. For as the heavens are higher than the earth, So are My ways higher than your ways and My thoughts than your thoughts.*
Even though His words soothed her, she was still perplexed but she would understand after while.
"Uncle John?" Her grandmother never married her boyfriend James but Chaya still liked to call him uncle because

Chaya's First Death

she'd done it since her youth. "When is this going to be over? I'm tired of sitting out here waiting for our turn."

"In a minute baby. In a minute. I just hope Judge Porter is as nice as she used to be. She used to do criminal cases only. Now she's overseeing family law as well."

"I guess I really figured that all judges handle any type of case. Kinda' like the only thing needed to be done was deciding between who's right and who's wrong."

"I wish it was that simple. Naw, they pretty much choose which type they handle in law school or something. Anyway, you might remember as a little girl, your mother and grandmother having to come up here. Do you?"

Chaya didn't want to tell her play uncle that those memories had been plaguing her for sometime now, the same ones that nearly sent her to the mental institution. "Yeah Unc' I remember. But you know what's so strange? It's the fact that both of them had to appear in court on my birthday. And even aunt Sadie too. Now here I am. On my birthday. What a way to spend it huh?"

"Well you know I guess I'm getting old because I never really payed attention to that, but you are right though..." He paused a minute and continued. "Chay' look at it like this. On that date, each time I had a case to try, I won! So keep a positive mindset and believe we are already winners, alright?"

"You got that right Uncle John. I believe it and I receive it in Jesus' name."

The attorney and his client smiled at one another. Both waiting to become what they envisioned just seconds ago, winners.

The door was opened and the courtroom refilled as soon as it was emptied.

"Baby girl? We up." Chaya could tell her Uncle John was a tad bit nervous.

"Fi-na-lly! You aw'right Unc? Remember what we talked

A. *Life* Gant

about?"

"What's that, sweetheart?"

"I can't believe you already forgot!" Chaya joked with her attorney to loosen him up, but partly too because she was nervous as well. "Remember Unc', we are already winners!"

The case was moving along smoothly. Joshua didn't want much of anything from Chaya. He wanted to make sure she allowed him visitation whenever he wanted and that was fine. The only thing he really wanted was for this divorce not to happen. Chaya was torn between two opinions and the Lord began to speak as always, bringing clarity to the situation.

"...If I am God and I am who I say I am, then follow Me. ...for I will Never put more on you than you can bear..."

"Council it seems as if your clients are indecisive about some things."

Looking at both Josh and Chaya, the Judge asked them what the problem was. Joshua shared his side of the story and Chaya returned the favor. The blame game would have been played for hours, had not Judge Porter stepped in, with the sound of the gavel.

"*Bam! Bam! Bam!*" Any harder, and all feared the solid wood would be useful for a potpourri dish.

"I see we have some issues here that apparently neither of your attorneys dealt with. So I am going to deal with them myself. I hate to see this type of thing come through my courtroom. You guys have a bright future ahead of you and I want to see you work it out. Have you been to some counseling?"

Both nodded in agreement.

"Well have you tried to reconcile?"

Mixed signals by way of shoulder shrugs answered her question and the judge became displeased with this childish display.

"The court will adjourn after a brief recess of one hour. We need to give these children some time so they can quit

Chaya's First Death

wasting mine. Hopefully the two of you can work something out, but if it don't work, you all come back to me, and I will grant this mess."

"Bam!"

During recess, the former couple, after debating awhile, came to the conclusion, that it would be best to depart and go their seperate ways. It hurt, but both believed that it was for the best. Now what would the Judge say? Or do?

Chaya's answer to her particular case would not come until he showed her His power in the others.

A. *Life* Gant

~~~*Delta's closing statement*~~~
Chapter Twenty-Seven

"Ms. Delta Smith, please step forward."

Judge Porter had a look of disgust on her face. She hadn't begun to understand why this seasoned woman stood before her.

"You have been found guilty and are being charged with wreckless use of an unauthorized firearm. Now before I deliver your sentence, I must remind you to remain quiet until I have finished. Is that understood?"

"Yes Ma'am."

"Bailiff, please get Ms. Smith a chair so that she can sit down. We don't want her leg to start hurting from standing too long."

He did as asked and Delta quietly thanked him.

"Ms. Delta Smith, you have come in my courtroom before because of your children and although this case has nothing to do with the former, there is an underlying current.

You, Delta are that underlying current. You have been there for folk when you didn't want to be. You are a giver of yourself and of your time, even when it wasn't deserved. I think I know why you do it, because you remind me a lot of my grandmother and she too walked in the same shoes you are now wearing. She, like you, loved the Lord and it was passed down from her mother as well. Both of you carry yourselves very well and I only aspire to do the same when I am older. I say this because you demand the same thing of your descendants, that they too, carry themselves in a way that is not only pleasing to

Chaya's First Death

you but pleasing to God. She kept her house clean and in order and I remember her telling me one time, as I have heard your children say also, that she truly believes cleanliness is next to godliness. Her children, although some have gone astray, were commanded to walk with their heads held high and their chests stuck out too, but the strange thing is that those types of life lessons are not given out as much as before and thank God that all your children and hers, have now gotten themselves together in some shape or form, because I know that you expect nothing less!

    I just have one thing that I want you to do different than my grandmother, and she would agree with me too, that you would not allow yourself to be used up 'til the point of death. That's one of the characteristics of an enabler. You can't take on everybody else's problems. You have enough of your own. So stop it and love on yourself. You deserve it!

    However, because of your incident, you will be placed on probation for three months and you can not carry your weapon until you get a permit. You must attend all the necessary classes that instructs the proper use of handguns. After you have completed them, you will report back to me, so that a copy of your license can be put on file.

    Now Delta, don't allow yourself to be put in positions where you become the one who suffers because of someone else's ignorance anymore. Do you understand me?"

"Yes Ma'am."

Ms. Smith, as I close your case, I would hope that you would leave those men who do nothing but take and take and take, alone. You are not to be used by anyone or anybody but the Lord... So let Him use you in which ever way he sees fit!

"Bam"

"The court is adjourned."

~184~

~~~Dinah's Closing Statement~~~
Chapter Twenty-Eight

"Miss Dinah Smith please step forward."

The judge smiled and shook her head at the young lady who stood before her.

"Miss Dinah Smith, you resemble your mother a lot, and it pains me to see one of her children in here right behind her, protecting something or someone that needed no protection at all!

Dinah, I see my own mother in you. She was something else too! As pretty as she wanted to be, but had a temper! She was a lot like you, both of you are quick to speak your mind knowing full well that trouble may soon follow. Momma's mouth was tough like yours but at the same time she was weak. I too, see your weakness. Not because you two couldn't wrestle with the boys and win, but you two are lovers and lovers wear their hearts on their sleeve. You try to cover up your sensitivities with strength and that's okay. But like my mother, you have to allow God's strength to be made perfect in your weakness..."

Judge Porter sighs and begins to tear up thinking about her own mother.

"Your weakness. Whew! Your weakness usually always have something to do with somebody else, mainly men and the love of them. If it had not been for that same love, you would not have to go through what you went through.

So Miss Dinah Smith, please do yourself a favor by taking that same love-filled strength and use it as a weapon against the enemy, to be a strong role model for your children.

Chaya's First Death

In the trying of your case, you had favor because your victim was stupid enough to try and file charges in a whole other state than where the crime happened and your case was dismissed. But!...You must learn from your mistakes and pay close attention to your friend. Do you know who I am talking about?"

Dinah knew she was speaking of Sadie and her now falling tears, gave the judge the answer to her a question.

"That could be you! As a matter of fact, it is you and you know it! But it is the you that didn't get caught. Just keep in mind that if it had not been for the Lord and your mother, on your side, helping you, the situations could be reversed. So Dinah never forget to thank the Lord for being the God of second chances!"

"Bam!"

The judge brought down the gavel as if she was upset but then again that was just how Mrs. Porter ruled, with a heart of passion.

"Court is adjourned."

~~~Sadie's Closing Statement~~~
Chapter Twenty-Nine

"Miss Sadie Edward's please step forward!"

"I really don't have much to fuss at you about because your punishment is and will be handed down for a long time to come. That's not to say you won't emerge from this victorious because you will, but until then, your sentence reads as follows:

For the next three months, you and your girls must attend family counseling. You must attend parenting classes yourself and make a weekly visit to see your designated therapist who will supervise you and your enactment with the children. You will be put on a strict curfew and must be in the house by ten p.m.. If you do not abide by these rules, you will be placed on house arrest! Do I make myself clear?"

"Yes Ma'am"

Sadie cried and could not believe she was being treated so harshly but she knew she deserved some of it. She would have been a better mother but she thought she was doing okay, despite her own upbringing, until now.

The judge could see the pain that this verdict was causing Sadie and she decided to finish it in her office.

"Miss Edward's I would like to see you in my chambers. Bailiff show her the way."

After the judge thanked him for escorting Sadie, she picked up her gavel to end court.

"Court is adjourned"

"Bam, Bam!"

Chaya's First Death

Judge Porter positioned two chairs to face each other and the ladies sat down. With Sadie's hand in hers, Mrs. Porter began...again.

"I believe that you may think that your sentence was a hard one, but it really isn't if you look at it in another light.

You have lost out on a lot of your girls' youth, all because you were running behind some man. And had you been home instead of gone so much, you may have been able to prevent what has happened to your child. Your little girl was searching for love that she could not find in you as a mother, even after she slept with the love of a man she longed for in a father.

Is there a father in the home, Miss Edwards?"

"No Ma'am."

Sadie teared up at the mention of the word 'home' because soon she may not have one.

"Well I am a living witness that God does move and work in the lives of a single-parent household. I am a product of that and not to brag or boast, look at me now! God did it! Not only for me, but for you. He did it so that I could be here to tell you it's going to be alright. What He did for me, He can and will do for you, but you must trust Him!

Miss Edwards, I'm going to let you in on a little secret. You are not the first and you certainly won't be the last woman to come through my courtroom because of some mess like this. You have to want to change and show your babies that there is a better way. You must give to them what was not given to you and you know what I am talking about don't you?"

"Yes Ma'am."

"What?"

"Love?"

"You are absolutely right. Sadie you take your babies by the hands of their hearts and you squeeze them until you can not squeeze anymore. Let those girls feel the love that God has given you so that they can know that somebody cares for them. You

A. *Life* Gant

have to be there with them, taking the necessary steps to freedom. The freedom to love and be loved, the right way.

Now if you should fall, get back up and keep going because God has promised, that if you allow Him to lead and guide you every step of the way, you'll make it! Guaranteed!"

The judge stood up to hug Sadie and told her she was free to leave, but just as she returned the chairs to their respectful places, she realized that her assignment was not yet complete.

"Oh yeah and Sadie?"

"Yes?"

"This was something God had me put together a couple of days ago and I didn't know who or what it was for but I do now."

The judge handed Sadie a beautiful wooden box that resembled the shape of a bible. In it held one of her favorite scripture-based readings called 'Footprints' and a check for two thousand dollars.

For Sadie, God did just what He said He would do...
HE SHOWED UP!!

Chaya's First Death

~~~*Chaya's Closing Statement*~~~
Chapter Thirty
20 years later!

    After the judge's unprecedented speeches and closing statements to Delta, Dinah and Sadie, it was now Chaya's turn and God was repositioning her restless, sleep-filled body. His hand caused her to cuddle up next to the edge of the headboard and by the looks of it, she was uncomfortable, but clefts do not always offer comfort, they provide protection!

    Both lawyers stated the resolutions of their clients. They let the judge know that the couple decided the best thing to do was part peacefully. The petitions were granted and the judge commanded all except Chaya to be seated. Everyone else in the room seemed invisible. Her judicial robe came off and she adorned herself with an angelic robe like that of a mother, a grandmother, an aunt, and the likes. At that moment she became whatever Chaya needed and the words she spoke were as a jet plane straight from heaven. Chaya stood there as still as she could because she believed that she already had the victory. But for some reason, her belief would become cemented by the words of Judge Aycee Porter.

    "Come here baby. I know you. I know where you come from. I know who your grandmother is. Her name is Delta and her daughter, Dinah, is your mother. Correct me if I am wrong."

    Chaya smiled and tears began to flow.

    "You look just like them and when you walked into my courtroom, my heart sank. I figured I was going to have to judge a case about some violence. You know they were a piece of work don't you?"

Chaya laughed through her tears and the judge couldn't help but laugh too, but her tune changed and her robe glowed ever so brightly.

"I know you. I know you because you are me. I know you because you are a lot of young women. I know you because you represent soo many people who are hurting out there...wondering why? Why me Lord? You ask those questions quite often. You want to know how I know? Because I ask those same questions myself and many folks do. They're just too afraid to admit it. Why does it seem like I am the only one going through this? Why do I have to hold my head up when I want to put it down? I want to cry but folk keep looking for me to be the strong one..."

Chaya could barely stand up. Every word the judge spoke was true, but for every tear, she could feel a little more strength because this verdict of words was much needed.

"...It's okay to cry Chaya. It's okay. You want to know why things happen to you that don't happen to anyone else? Let me share some things with you for a minute..."

Chaya was flabbergasted at the way this judge was speaking to her and her mind began to wander.

"Do all judges talk to you like they are really this concerned, like a parent would?"

She wondered but dared to interrupt this judge because actually, she felt that every question she had ever asked, was on the verge of being answered.

"Miss Chaya are you still listening? I am almost done."

"Yes Ma'am."

"You may be wondering why I handle certain cases the way I do, well I'm getting ready to tell you and I want you to listen and listen well..."

Chaya's feet were starting to hurt. She had been standing for what seemed like eternity, but sneaking a peek at the clock

Chaya's First Death

told her only fourteen minutes had passed. The pain subsided when Mrs. Porter had told her to listen. Those words reminded her of her grandmother and made her stand a little taller. When grandma used to say that, usually something important followed.

"I don't just sit on this bench to decide the fate of people's lives. I have worked hard for years to be able to function properly in this position, and because of that, I believe God sent me here to help those in need of an emotional healing. Chaya most people get in trouble because of an emotional need. They lost control of the situation and figured they would take it back. But in most cases, it is too late. I say this because it is not too late for you. You don't have to be a product of your environment any longer. Your mother and grandmother were codependents, you have been up until now, and the title you once held as an enabler is now done away with."

The Judge disappeared in Chaya's eyes and became as if it were God Himself in a light that blinded her yet kept her standing strong.

"Chaya, outside of these four walls and in church I am not only known as the Judge, but the Chain Breaker. I have been authorized and deputized to stop and break, any, and every, generational curse that comes my way. You learned to be as you were because that is what you saw. You saw the female role models in your life make it easy for another person, male or female, to continue and persist in self-destructive behavior. They provided excuses for the ones they loved and in doing so, they made it possible for that person or persons to avoid consequences of such behavior. No longer can I or will I allow this to be so. The curse may have halted and stopped with them but as I bring down this gavel, my decision in the case concerning you and the verdict that has been reached will now be made available for all to see, so that they can run with it, and know, that every generational curse doesn't just stop with me, it has to be **broken**!...."

"BANG! BANG! BANG!"

A. *Life* Gant

"...each hit representing that **IT IS SO!**

The words of the Judge assassinated her former being. She would no longer be an enabler. Everyone of her family members, friends, and all connected to her in some way, would now stand on their own two feet, and she would enjoy the show. Sitting down! The weight of the lives of others had to be carried by its owners. Her back was free! Never to be loaded down again. Not by means of self or anyone else. And for the first time in a long time, Chaya slept. But even more than that, she *rested*!

~~~~~~~~~~~~

Habakkuk 2:2-3
...Write the vision, and make it plain upon tables, that he may run that readeth it. For the vision is yet for an appointed time, but at the end it shall speak, and not lie: though it tarry wait for it; because it will surely come...

Jeremiah 29:11
...For I know the thoughts that I think toward you, saith the Lord, thoughts of peace, and not of evil, to give you an expected end.

About the Author

A. Gant, is a mother, an author, and an entrepreneur. She was born and raised in the state of Oklahoma, where she now resides with her family. She is currently working on another novel titled <u>Secret Wounds and Hidden Pain</u>. When she is not writing, she is working in the Health and Beauty industry, where she is first; a salon owner and operator, developing hair products and second; a personal trainer.

Gant has always loved to write and has written numerous pieces yet to be discovered. She believed she had something to share with the world through her writings, about overcoming emotional struggles and internal issues. Thus, her debut novel, <u>Chaya's First Death, The Beginning of an End to her life as an Enabler</u>, was birthed, with a name switch. Both her actual first name and Chaya (pronounced; k-eye-a) have the same meaning and from this, her alias ***'Life'***, was created.